RIPSKILLIAN TALES

Written by David Driver

Best wishes

David Driver

Sunflowers for Laura, Snake Boy and Singles Club were first published as an ebook, under the title All Things Bright and Beautiful. Desert People, For Sale and The Beggar were first published as an ebook, under the title Ripskillian.

David Driver was born, and still lives, in Yorkshire. He shares his life with his beautiful wife Rosalind, two daughters, Stefanie and Mollie, Betty the dog, various cats, a bearded dragon, a couple of guinea pigs and some chickens. Places of escape include Whitby, Cornwall and Turkey. One day he hopes to visit Japan. You can follow David on Twitter; David Driver@GingerScribbler. Or alternatively you can leave a review or comment on Facebook, Red Head Books or Facebook m.facebook.com/thewritersbookshelf.

Other titles by the same author

Paperbacks

Devilishly Dandelicious Poems
(Written under the name Arthur G. Mustard)

The Weird Wonderful Unique and Unusual Lives of Everyday People

The Purple Orchid of Ulysses Goyle

About Akiko Kobayashi

Akiko Kobayashi is a brilliantly talented artist who was born in Tarumi-ku Kobe-shi, Hyogo, Japan. After surviving The Great Hanshin-Awaji Earthquake and bullying at school, I am pleased to say that she didn`t give up and continued to pursue her lifelong dream of becoming a worldwide recognised artist.We came together by pure chance via social media and I cannot thank her enough for all her hard work and efforts in contributing to this book. Akiko has brought some of my characters and ideas to life using her wonderful skills as an artist. Thank you. If you would like to know more about her or look at more of her work, please visit;

Gallery site @http://akiko-kobayashi.pixels.com/

Facebook @https://facebook.com/akikonpeitou

Linkedin @https://www.linkedin.com/profile/view?id=338371185

Contents

Sunflowers for Laura

Life`s been hard in the city these last few months, hard in the city of Roth. We had won the war, defeated the invading Vemish and everything seemed good for a short time. But then there`s not much use for a soldier, not much work, when the war`s over. It`s difficult to start to learn how to farm, or run a market stall. Life`s tougher still when the King raises taxes to pay for *his* glorious victory. People "close ranks", so to speak, look after their own, forget who kept them free and allowed them to speak their native tongue.

ΔΔΔ

I`ll never forget that summer morning, blue sky, cloudless, flowers blooming, birds singing. Dressed in black leather boots, brown leather trousers and matching tunics, our clean pressed, white shirts bore the King`s twin eagled crest. We marched towards the city gates, cheers, applause and shouts of victory filled the air.

And there they stood, Ella my wife and Laura, our daughter; both beautiful, my life, my reason for living. Ella waved; smiling, blue eyes full of love, soft, long red hair adorned with daisies and standing at her side an exact image of her mother apart from her "sunflower" hair, Laura, our four year old daughter. She was holding a small sunflower between her tiny white hands, twirling it, smelling it. A smile spread across her innocent, warm fresh face.

Eyes sparkled. "Daddy, daddy," Laura`s voice engulfed me with happiness. Waving the flower like a flag, she spoke again, excited. "Daddy, I love you."

Marching in unison, swords at our sides, muskets slung over shoulders, we moved forward. Stopping, whilst the mighty gates opened, salutes were made and cheers erupted.

All our eyes met and I mimed the words, "Love you both." Ruffling Laura`s hair, I pretended to steal her nose. She gave me the sunflower, which was quickly tucked away inside my tunic.

Belching open with dust, groans and creaks, the twenty foot high wooden gates revealed the striking landscape; lush, green grass, red, yellow, pink and white flowers. Mighty oaks, elms and beech housed the denizens of the woodland. Evergreens dotted the slopes, becoming more in number higher up the trails and beyond, the orange, black and grey of the mountains were capped with the occasional wisp of a cloud. The calming, smooth flow of the river relaxed our minds as we began the long journey. Clear, fresh water glistened under the full red, simmering heat of the sun.

That was the beginning, the start of long marches, hot days, cool nights and new friendships. Captain and cook weren`t bad, so at least we didn`t have to eat typical army slop after listening to some rich, high ranking officer`s son.

Captain Henry Fariner had wealth, but saw life at our level. Charlie Pedler, or Chicken Lips as he became known, could make anything taste good and we always seemed able to march a few extra miles on what we ate. Good old Chicken Lips, I think he`s dead now. Got his name when someone cracked a joke about how he could even cook the lips of a chicken. Good shot too with a musket and didn`t hesitate to put the blade into the Vemish. It was said that every soldier always kept an eye out for Charlie in battle, rather than the flag bearer, anyone could pick up the King`s banner.

We kept going, survived, lived to fight another day, drove the invaders back. This was *our* land, not those red eyed savages from across the waters. Sharp features, dark skinned, vast numbers, their blood always seemed thicker, redder when it ran.

Good friends were made and good friends were lost during the three years we fought in the King`s army. Even saved the Captain`s life twice, said he could do with more men like me.

All through the long, bloody three years, I kept the sunflower Laura had given me. Towards the end of the first week it began to wilt. Fariner saw me looking at the dying flower, asked where it came from, took it away, pressed it, then returned my precious, yellow gift. He said he had a daughter back home the same age as Laura, smiled and returned to the officers` tents.

Victory eventually became ours; we even burnt some of the ships, sinking them to the depths of the Iord Sea. Only a thousand, at the most, survived and fled.

The men of Roth returned that autumn as heroes, loved,

revered. Unmarried soldiers soon were, and the rest of us held our loved ones again, including me.

ΔΔΔ

It felt so good to hold them once more. Crying, looking, touching, I couldn't believe how much Laura had changed, how much she had grown. Ella looked as beautiful as ever, no different from the day I left.

That night, her soft, smooth skin felt good against mine. The scent of her body, the sound of her voice, the touch of her lips, all soothed the empty, blood stained nights. I awoke that first morning to the smell of fresh bread, bacon and eggs. Ella smiled, Laura jumped on the bed, talking endlessly as I ate.

We still lived in the small cottage next to the bakery and life seemed normal again. The war was over, money was plentiful and I had three years to catch up on. There's not much to spend army pay on when you just sleep, march, eat and fight.

Along with a small share of Vemish spoils, an unexpected bonus, we considered ourselves quite wealthy; new boots for me, along with cotton shirts and leather waistcoats and beautiful dresses for my girls. I was offered a job game keeping for one of the rich landowners. The fresh air was good, I wasn't a bad shot and also helped "sort out" the poachers and rogues who wandered onto the land.

But eight months down the line, things changed and we started to pay the price of war. Victory and glory belonged to the King, but the royal purse was empty. *He* needed to rebuild, strengthen his defences, replace lost troops and confirm his wealth and power in the land. Money was needed and slowly but surely taxes were raised. People's pockets were soon drained, work dwindled and unrest spread. The rich landowner no longer needed me, my hands were not for farming and the market traders paid very little.

We lost the cottage, couldn't pay the rent and moved into the small room above the bakery. Ella looked tired, Laura's clothes were tattered and sometimes her wooden vase had to go empty. Laura had always loved flowers, especially sunflowers. They always grew in numbers, during the summer, in the fields by the river. During this

10.

time the vase never went empty, always a yellow circle of petals, always a smiling face of happiness, that's how the summer went.

But along with the rent, bread, meat, clothes and everything else, the precious sunflowers carried a heavy price. Daisies and dandelions replaced the favourite bringer of endless smiles, as we couldn't afford them. Even flowers such as these were seen as a wealth provider and guards were posted around the fields.

Unrest spread, violence grew and the dark corners of the city became blood stained. Thieves and murderers were hung, lesser crimes received a severe flogging and at that time the army seemed a fairer place.

Whilst Laura slept, Ella and I talked. Should we go? Where? How? We have no money. And when only my eyes were open, I lay, holding the pressed sunflower, the occasional tear escaping.

Sometimes I stood, looking at them, sometimes I looked beyond the walls and imagined better things, but always I returned to now. Returned to now and at that present moment it wasn't good.

ΔΔΔ

Everything seemed to fall apart in one day, events, people, places, all seemed wrong. After breakfast, I took a walk through the market, hoping to find something that wasn't there. All seven colours of the rainbow filled the flowers on the stall, along with twice as many scents. Sat there, right in the middle, sunflowers stared at me. But it was simple, no money, no flowers.

Then I saw the leather purse, a fat wealthy merchant moved two steps ahead and my eye caught a snatcher disappearing into the crowd. He must have cut it loose, fumbled, then left before the guards seized him. As I straightened, the words "Sir, I think you dropped this," touched my lips. But the merchant turned, took in, drew his own conclusions and the guards grabbed *my* arms.

Things moved quickly and before long I was there, there in the ten foot square cell; cold stone floor and walls, straw in the corner for a bed and a wooden bucket for my personal use. Black iron bars caged me in, the dimly lit passage faded into the distance and torches flickered in sconces. A small, barred window looked out into the yard below. Voices echoed, odours scented and cries of pain sounded, as certain inmates received a good "sticking". The pleasures of Benith jail were always in abundance.

My name is William Birch, twenty eight years old. I`d served six years in the King`s army and would serve only about a week in the cells before been hung by the neck.

Six, eight days at the most, that`s all it takes. Once you were arrested, the King and his council met, to discuss you, talked about you, decided your fate. You just sat and waited, waited `till they came and led you out to the gallows in the square below.

"Special guests" were taken out to the crossroads to swing and when they`d stopped kicking, they became a feast for the crows. But at least if you were hung in the square, your loved ones could collect and bury you.

No one ever went free, not any commoner that is. One man walked though, a rapist. Rumour had it he was related to the King`s cousin and went away to lands in the north.

Ella and Laura came to the yard on the first and second day. Both were dressed in their best dresses and Laura was carrying sunflowers. My face pressed against the bars as I looked down. But my cell was three floors up, so voices didn`t carry too well. Fingers reached through, waving. Ella did the same and Laura held the flowers aloft. The following days became empty, as if I`d already met the gallows. No sight of either my wife or daughter. Even the third floor jailor, Mathew Cork, had suddenly disappeared.

Mathew Cork, not a bad man, mid-fifties, one eye, bad breath and portly. Served in the army himself many years ago, said he had a knack of knowing a good man from a bad one. Cork seemed to like me for some reason, knew I was innocent. "Sorry lad," he said. "A know yer no thief, can see it in yer eyes. But shite, a commoner won`t walk."

Before he`d vanished, Cork had stood staring through the bars, passed me several cigars and a bottle of brandy, smiled, turned and walked away with his usual gait. Another cell door opened, two, maybe three men rushed in. A man cried out as the beating started, Cork had said they had another murderer in. Closing my eyes, I was thankful I hadn`t had the pleasure of a "sticking".

12.

The only conversation I had now was with myself. Still no sign of Cork, he`d been replaced; a deaf mute brought my food, stared, then left. The second cigar was good and the brandy excited my senses as it flowed down my throat.

My eyes were bleary and kept closing for minutes at a time, sleep was just about upon me. *Never mind, who cares?* I thought. I wished I could hold them again, hear their voices, see their smiles. *Ella, Laura, what are you doing? Please be with me in this cell.*

My eyes slowly opened, narrow slits, suddenly springing open wide, bewildered. A tall, cloaked figure stood over me within the cell. Backing away, not standing, I reached the far wall. My eyes kept with those of the man I recognized.

Black robes, red cord trimmed the edges, pristine, black leather boots, sharp, hawk like features, grey, swept back hair lightly covered a balding head. Piercing, brown eyes stared out from the pale face. The gold ring of The Order of Prayer sat on the third finger of the left hand. No muscle weighed on the weak frame, but this old man carried power and fear within Roth. Oh yes, I *had* seen this man before.

On the day we marched off to war, he had blessed us, told us we fought in the name of The Order and Faith. He had visited various camps before battle, repeating the same words. Only the King, and *possibly* several other men, carried more power than The Head of the Order of Prayer, the true and only religion.

Every condemned man received a visit from the Order before he died, whether it was a novice or higher. And none came higher than the visitor I had received, High Priest Aspin Bead. Feared, loathed, hated, revered, he now stood over me, the ex-soldier.

After three hard swallows, I found little spit and slowly gathered my words. "Sir, I mean High Priest." Bead just stood and stared. "I`ve tried to be a good man, love and protect my family." Continuing, I told of my family, my time in the army and my loyalty to the King. I told of the hardships I had faced on my return, protested my innocence, but accepted my fate.

Aspin Bead never spoke, never moved, never showed *any*

emotion. He just stood, staring, fingering his thin moustache with a forefinger. As the condemned "war hero" continued, me, a thought came to mind about a saying in the slums amongst the thieves. *When in the cell and the visitor is Bead, say your prayers, the gallows call, your neck 'll stretch for the greed.*

I must have fallen asleep again, eyes flew open, thoughts raced. Scrambling to my feet, I realized I was alone in the cell. Bead was gone.

Reaching the window, my eyes scanned the yard below. Laura stood alone, holding sunflowers, my heart raced. Footsteps sounded, followed by a voice and I snapped out of my trance.

"Birch, Birch." Mathew Cork spoke.

Turning round, our eyes met and I replied. "Mathew, Mathew Cork."

"Aye, that`s me lad."

"Come to get me then. Well, never mind, we both knew the outcome. Spoke to Bead last night. "

"Bead? What y` talking about? Bead. Too much brandy, knew a should`ve drunk it meself. "

"He came last night, to see me. I spoke with him. "

"Never thought ad see it, never, a commoner go free."

I stood and stared, Cork continued. "Yer must `a` bin a damn good soldier, a said that *you* wer` a good man. Yer wer` gonna swing, no two ways, until that Lord Fariner turned up. "

"Lord Fariner? "

"Aye lad, Lord Fariner. But *you* remember `im as Captain Fariner. Spoke up, real posh. `is father died last year, got lot, land, money, title, all down south west. Lots a powerful folk `av` bin about last few days, talking, sorting things out. Lord Fariner stood up, spoke to t` King, said more men like *you* wer` needed. Said all that when he found out about yer in jail. Told t` King *you* saved `im, more than once and he owed yer. King listened. Fariner said he needed *you* on *his* lands, to help wi` rogues. *You* and yer family can travel wi` `im, leave the city. Free Birch, yer free lad."

Emotion swept over me, tears welled, legs weakened and I became dizzy. Cork opened the cell door, entered, placed a hand on my shoulder and spoke. "Yer best get gone lad, before a get meself a bad name."

Coughing a laugh, my thoughts raced. "Yes, I`ll go. Thanks Mathew. But…but what, no you`re right, too much brandy, a dream. I don`t know." As the words came, I eyed the empty bottle.

    Leaving the cell, I took several steps, then turned and spoke. "So Mathew, where`ve you been these past days?"

"Aye lad, never told yer did a. Took me ower t` see King`s private jail. Had t` watch a special prisoner. King`s bin after this murderer fer years. All Lords wer` there, all ones that `av` a say. Lots a scandal. Found `im guilty, good, foul scum. Hung `im, good `n` proper. Hung `im at` crossroads fer what he did, yesterday morning. Killed lots a people, always woman `n` girls. Yer won`t believe this lad, so just let me tell yer. Man who swung, Aspin Bead. Aspin Bead, murderer."

    "Aspin Bead?" Staggering, almost fainting, I reached for the wall.

"That`s right. Caught `im, knife in hand, covered in blood, victims barely cold. Over by a bakery four days ago, mother `n` daughter. Little `un dressed in pink `n` holding sunflowers. "

Snake Boy

I thought I`d never return to India after 1857, but I was wrong. Five of us kept in touch after the rebellion, Charlie, Jimmy, White Eye, Hans and me. One big family we were and Hans was the biggest, all six foot seven of him. He came back to London with us, said he had no family back home. We made a good living working at the docks. But we made more money from the illegal prize fighting arranged by White Eye. Hans won every time in the heavyweight bouts, whilst Charlie, Jimmy and myself held our own amongst the lighter divisions.

Charlie and Jimmy were the first to hear about the expedition; our luck seemed to change quite quickly and for the worse. Lord Beamsley, a young man, was funding and leading the venture, whilst our old Major was recruiting men with army experience.

Major Golding remembered each one of us, even seemed pleased to see us and we were all put on the payroll. We left in two weeks` time from Charing Cross, where the train would take us as far as Folkestone; from here we would cross the Channel and land in Boulogne. From here it became too complicated for me; a mixture of more train journeys, sailing under the power of steam and something involving the Mahmoudieh Canal.

Lord Beamsley had everything in order; people speaking different languages, people waiting on arrival, accommodation and all the necessary documents. This suited me fine, as I was earning, traveling, eating well and laughing amongst friends.

One of the ship`s crew fancied his chances against Hans, so we made a little money. The Major himself made sure it was a clean fight and even Lord Beamsley had a flutter. He said afterwards that boxing was a good sport for a man and sorted out differences in a British way.

ΔΔΔ

The Port of Calcutta looked all too familiar and memories came flooding back. Setting foot once more on *old* ground, we all shared a joke. The red coats which sent fear into the hearts of past enemies

16.

were gone, but the rifles remained; Enfield Patterns and they felt good.

Horses, tents, supplies and guides had all been arranged by Lord Beamsley. Most of us spoke a little of the language, so no barriers were formed. The only people that didn`t seem to fit in were the Professor and his team.

Five of them in all and each one thought that *they* were leading the expedition. They were so called "experts"; educated men who would tell us how to track and capture the animals, or carefully pick the plants and flowers.

We soon fell into a routine and the days became weeks. Plants and flowers were easy to collect, along with some of the smaller animals. The locals were happy to take them back to the ship and everything seemed to flow along nicely.

Tigers were plentiful, but savage. Four men died on our first encounter and even the Major took a blow to the leg. But the snakes were the ones to watch out for. Short, long, colourful, slithering, I hated them.

The locals knew which the most deadly ones were. I believe they even revered them. In the grass, under stones, coiled around branches, these reptiles seemed to be everywhere.

I`ll never forget the night when savage lightning put fear into all of us, enough rain fell to fill an empty lake; no one slept. By dawn, the sun shone and the sky was a cloudless blue. Not a drop of rain in sight.

After breakfast we set out, travelling deeper into the jungle. The Professor became excited after finding some sort of exotic plant. But then things turned bloody when Charlie was killed.

Suddenly screaming, he fell, writhing in pain. Racing to help, we all hesitated, turning pale. I open fired and the rest followed. Rifles sounded as the giant reptile was peppered with bullets.

All fifteen foot of green and brown scaled muscle lay motionless. The two foot thick body trickled with crimson blood and amber eyes just glared. Voices sounded and arguments broke out, as the Professor and his team said we were savages who should learn to think and not act with our rifles.

Fangs had struck Charlie's neck, puncturing the skin. Two gaping holes oozed blood and venom. His face was twisted with fear.

White Eye and myself spoke. We'd carry Charlie's body back to camp and give him a decent burial. The others didn't know, but soon would.

That evening, Lord Beamsley and Major Golding said a few words and Charlie was buried. A few hours later the camp was divided into four. The Professor and his team were talking about the possibility of more giant reptiles, the locals were considering leaving, ourselves, who were full of brandy and memories, leaving only the Lord and *his* men.

News travelled fast and soon most knew about the snake we had encountered. The loyal men of the village stayed and we divided into two. Half returned to the ship, as most of the collection was complete. Myself, Hans, White Eye, along with the Major and about twelve others, travelled deep into the jungle.

Two died to the deadly venom, another when we crossed a small lake. He was dragged under by the water loving serpent, spoiling the picturesque scene of calm blue water with his blood and backpack which both floated to the surface.

Fear set in, they knew we were coming, getting closer, nearing *their* lair. We should have shot the Professor and his team. They seemed to care more for the snakes than they did for the rest of us.

ΔΔΔ

Hans and myself saw him, *him who should be dead,* first. The jungle cleared, rocks and fallen trees lay motionless and that now familiar stench fouled the air, snakes.

The sight froze us both; wonder, awe, fear and resentment filled our bodies. Breathing slowed as we both glanced at each other and then at the sight before us. A boy, no more than ten, just sat there. Naked, black haired, seated within a half shell of a snake's egg, he stared right back in to our eyes.

His human form housed the same amber eyes of the cold blooded denizens of this cursed land. Scaled, mottled flesh covered his legs and after a minute or so just staring, they seemed to merge as one, resembling that of these fanged jungle dwellers.

Rifle ready, all I had to do was squeeze, but the Major appeared and all changed. When everyone had stared, we snared the little juvenile viper.

No words escaped his mouth, only hissing, coupled with a forked tongue. Two died as he struck with deadly speed, the poison acting instantly. He had the strength of a grown man for one who looked so young, but we managed to cage him within the wooden prison.

More snakes struck as we began our return journey. The Major kept order as we travelled quickly and lightly through the hellish surroundings, leaving those who had fallen.

Only six returned; the Major, Hans, White Eye, two of the Professor`s men and of course me. We all took turns to carry the wooden cage which housed *him*. Him, the spawn of evil which should have been left in that cursed part of jungle, where man was never meant to tread.

Frenzy, panic and superstition spread like a forest fire at the height of June. According to the locals we were taking away a God, a sacred piece of their country and tensions were high. Only a few of the locals remained with us and Hans and myself had to disperse a mob bent of freeing our new found prize.

Some of us talked of killing the boy, this Snake Boy, or Shesha as the locals called him. Charlie was dead, along with others and we wanted a little retribution; it wasn`t right, it wasn`t natural. Maybe we could just set him free, but Lord Beamsley overheard our conversation.

Money, wealth, whatever you want to call it, can be a powerful persuader and Lords can be very persuasive. After he`d finished, we had a sample of the money which would come our way.

He didn`t give names, but spoke of people in London who had influence. They wanted to open exhibition halls, hold lectures, tour the country and visit universities. These people could hold the civilised world to ransom and we could be a part of it. All we had to do was keep quiet, hold our nerve and protect the ship and its cargo. Two days, that`s all we had left in foreign lands and then we were bound for England.

Supplies were collected within the now hostile environment, but again money spoke with twice the normal price changing hands. We set sail, but two days into the journey and death called once more. White Eye`s life was claimed by Snake Boy. The dead body lay slumped against the bars. Hans and myself had the same idea, but knew Lord Beamsley would have us both shot if we reached for our rifles.

Stomachs retched when we turned White Eye to face us. Torn flesh and blood surrounded the empty eye socket. Snake Boy had ripped out the glass eye and now half hid it within the clothes we had given him.

Our dead friend had lost his eye at sixteen, when only his second shot with a rifle backfired. An old Chinese man, dead now, carried out the work thirteen years ago.

A trio remained, Hans, myself and Jimmy. Months passed and England drew nearer. Snake Boy seemed to grow, appear older. We set up shifts, taking turns to throw him rats and watch through rifle sights. It seemed strange that we fed the rats to keep them alive, took them out of their cages and threw them to Snake Boy to keep him alive. But then again, I suppose nothing seemed strange to us now.

The final leg eventually came, Calais to Plymouth; Lord Beamsley had arranged it personally. When the word, "Land," was spoken, we seemed to find new strength, even a smile. The coastline became visible to all, our coastline, England.

ΔΔΔ

The docks of Plymouth were *very* familiar, sounds, smells and sights. People were waiting, Lord Beamsley`s people, all armed and ready with horses, carts and even a carriage.

Shouts, arms waving, bodies running here and there, all contributed to the cargo been unloaded. Everything went smoothly and soon we were stood with nothing to do. An armed guard accompanied the "special" crate, each bearing Lord Beamsley`s family crest.

More money came our way as the Major took us all to a nearby tavern, where we ate and drank. We were told to come out to

Beamsley's estate in a week's time and Jimmy knew the way.

We lived like Lords ourselves, drinking, eating, laughing, buying new clothes and tasting the pleasures of women. But seven days soon pass and it was time to visit Lord Beamsley.

Remembering the Lord's men back at the docks, we rode to the estate, taking rifles and pistols just in case. If trouble was coming, we'd go down fighting.

The welcome we received wasn't what we had expected. Food and drink were plentiful, along with good conversation. Lord Beamsley seemed pleased to see us all again, along with the Major who had arrived three days ago.

Others were there, including the Professor. Rich gentlemen from around the world were gathered; French, German, Indian, Dutch, even a married couple all the way from America.

It was becoming clear that Lord Beamsley was indeed an intriguing and colourful character. Apart from been wealthy and influential, his reputation and friendships spanned the world. This gathering must have been planned months in advance.

Jimmy seemed happy to talk to the Americans. They were desperate to hear more about our adventures in India and longed to know how we captured Shesha, or Snake Boy as *we* had named him.

Hans and myself took a walk around the estate, discovering many new and strange things. Beasts from around the world, once fierce and majestic, now stood in glass trophy cabinets, stuffed and lifeless. Another room contained an array of weaponry, some crude, others elegant. A greenhouse played host to a multitude of exotic plants and fruits. Then we entered a room that changed everything.

It was cold from the moment we stepped inside, we both felt as if we were been watched and trod carefully on the wooden floor. Two cabinets stood, one to the left and one to the right. As I looked through the glass, words eluded me, an icy shiver stabbed my spine, engulfing my whole body and the *human* trophy stared back.

Embalmed, holding a beautifully decorated sword and wearing a colourful suit of armour, the eastern warrior posed menacingly within the confines of the glass. Hans also looked on in horror; the black, athletic tribesman threatened with his spear, but was never going to shatter the glass.

What the hell was this place? What sort of man was Lord Beamsley? We`d heard people talking about him, talking about his next venture. He planned to go to Brazil. Would he want us to go with him? Would we bring back trophies like these?

We returned to Jimmy, had a few drinks and told him the news. What had we got involved in? Me and Hans followed the Professor, whilst Jimmy circulated amongst the guests keeping an eye out.

They made their way to the south of the estate. Turning, smiling and seeming quite pleased to see us all again, the Professor invited us to join him. He said an old friend was waiting and we knew who it was.

The black iron gates swung open and we descended thirty stone steps. Another gate opened and we walked the cobbled floor of a short passage, before entering a large, dimly lit room. As the oak door closed, we knew what dwelt within.

Scarlet curtains were swept back to reveal iron bars and there *he* was, seated behind, Snake Boy. Instantly recognizing each one of us, he remained on the floor. But his pupils dilated as he looked into our very souls, haunting, hypnotic.

"Throw him a rat, for old time`s sake." As he spoke, the Professor laughed, carrying out his own instruction. Snake Boy struck with deadly speed, swallowing the animal whole. Two guards entered and started to tease the caged "prize" with a stick.

"You`re going to the Capital tomorrow freak, so all those lovely people can pay good money for a long look," one of the guards sneered as he spoke.

But then something strange happened. Snake Boy looked at me, not like before, but like a small, lonely child in need of help. I moved nearer, almost touching the bars and he held my gaze whilst rising to his feet.

From within his clothing he produced the white eye he had taken from our friend and gently placed it within my own hand. Hans saw what had happened. Closing my fingers around the gift, I closed my eyes.

Hans smiling was the view when I opened them. The butt of his

22.

rifle knocked the Professor to the ground unconscious. Seconds passed, a left hook sent one of the guards to the floor and then Han`s rifle pressed against the others cheek, before he could respond to my boxing prowess.

After that, everything happened so quickly. Three people stood outside the cell and three people were within. Bound and gagged they lay helpless. But we were also helpless, helpless because of the third person who stood alongside us.

We carefully reached the top of the stairs. How would we escape? There was a small iron gate within the wall, padlocked. Snake Boy broke the lock as if it were rotten wood. A plan quickly formed and we set to work.

Woodland lay beyond the gate, dense woodland, perfect for thieves to hide. Hans started a fire down in the cells and I smashed some of the cabinets, taking various weapons. Most of the people were talking and drinking in the west grounds, so we had plenty of time.

Smoke and flames soon belched up, I fired a shot and Lord Beamsley`s men came running. People were now everywhere, they found the weapons which I had dropped just beyond the gate and scattered into the woods in search of the intruders.

In all the commotion, the rest was easy. Hans found Jimmy, both gathered the horses and then we were mounted and away. No one questioned who the person was slung over my shoulder. He was now dressed in a guard`s uniform and thought to be suffering from smoke inhalation.

By the time the true facts had come to light, all four of us were hidden within the mighty London. Slums, sewers, abandoned buildings all became our homes. Days, weeks, eventually months passed.

A person like Lord Beamsley does not give up, he keeps on searching; he hunts us. I still don`t know why we did what we did. Was it a moment of madness, or Snake Boy`s will?

ΔΔΔ

He has become powerful and now speaks our tongue. He watches, learns and adapts. Rats are off the menu, he craves for something else, human flesh.

Nearly a year has passed and we mostly live in the sewers. Hundreds have fallen under his spell, working for him, carrying out his demands. Failure results in death. He has grown, appearing as a handsome man of twenty five with a liking for the ladies. He sometimes dwells within a large house located in the centre of London. Wealthy woman visit him here. That`s where the evil continues to spread and people continue to suffer.

All women fall under his spell, wealthy or whore. But most are hideously murdered and then devoured. I`m often sent to fetch the whores to satisfy his cravings. Men also suffer the same fate, but do not share his bed.

I cannot resist him, he controls my mind. Hans is half mad and has taken to speaking mostly German and eating rats. Our *master* mocks him, laughing, hissing and pointing.

Jimmy is dead, killed by our reptilian captor when he tried to escape. Hans tried to help and was blinded; blinded by the venom spat into his eyes by the Serpent King, who laughed menacingly at his actions with pure delight.

On the streets of London they talk of Lord Beamsley. He is crippled, confined to a wheelchair. Who carried out such an attack? They ask. Only we know down in the sewers.

The Major is dead. Again tongues wagged. He will eventually kill them all, leaving the Lord until last, but slowly making him suffer. I believe we shall all die when no longer needed. No one can stop him, he is too powerful. We should have never brought him here. He belongs in his own land, where he was born to serve another purpose.

The people of his homeland knew who he was. They revered him, worshipped him. Shesha, King of the Serpents they called him. But we shall also know him, fear him and fall under his spell. We shall all succumb to the one we found in an egg, caged and named Snake Boy.

Singles Club

One big fat geek! That`s how I saw myself; From the age of ten I`d always been fat. I blamed my mother. "Eat your food John. There`s a good boy John. Would you like your pudding now John? I`ve got some chocolates for later John, we`ll share them." Those words of hers repeated in my head constantly.

I`ve never met my dad, only seen a few photos. He doesn`t look fat, he looks pretty cool. He looks like a rock star from the seventies. I bet he had plenty of women chasing him and never struggled for a shag.

They were never married, they didn`t even live together. Mind you, I`m not surprised! Mother tells me it was "pure love" for just one night. It happened in my dad`s room above The Red Lion. He`d taken mother back there after she`d been to see him sing with his band. There are a few photos lying around and I suppose she doesn`t look that bad. Mind you she was a lot thinner then.

Only a few "mates" came round to tea after school. The football team was a non-starter and girlfriends were just a part of my imagination. A job at Woolworths followed five GCSEs and I enrolled at college to study computer programming and business management.

The first time I plucked up any sort of courage to walk into a pub and order my first pint ended in disaster. Two lads, in the year above me at school, smacked me in the mouth and nicked one of my shoes whilst I was in the toilet. I even got chased through the bus station by a group of girls who had constantly teased me at school.

But then one Christmas, things changed. *"Coming in the New Year, Singles Club,"* it read. Singles Club? What`s that? I asked myself these questions. And after several minutes gawping through the window, I found out.

"Oh excellent! A Singles Club," glancing to my right, I listened as the large lady continued.
"What a wonderful idea young man. A chance to meet new people and who knows, maybe have a little romance." Before I knew it, a

second lady had joined the first and both indulged in conversation. The six forty five bus was due, so I came away from my *new* discovery.

Getting home, mother greeted me in the usual manner. Tomorrow would be Christmas Eve and Me and mother would share it in the same way we had always done.

ΔΔΔ

By the time December the twenty ninth came, I was bloated with turkey and chocolate Brazil nuts. A trip into the city reignited my encounter with the Singles Club. January the third was the official opening date and something inside my head told me I would be there.

Mother didn't mind. I told her not to wait up, but knew she would. The bus journey seemed quicker than usual, but then it didn't stop at every stop. Money was short until the masses received their next pay packet, so the city was only half alive. Only the lonely were out, only the saddos, only the singletons.

On the third time I passed the club, I made a decision to actually enter on the fifth. How shall I enter? Shall I make eye contact with people? What drink shall I order? Too many questions!

About a dozen or so people were inside. The large fat lady and her friend were there, two young lads, who were probably there for a laugh and an old man who clothes looked fashionable when the Titanic sank. The rest were just everyday sad lonely people, just like me.

So there I was, a half pint of bitter ordered, no eye contact made and I'd entered on my own two feet. Other people came, small, large, thin, old and young, but all single.

With no introduction, a slim woman in her fifties rose and began to speak. Her name was Mrs West. I found her quite attractive, but wasn't too keen on her heavy makeup and imitation posh voice.

We all listened, some intently, others only half interested. Some had obviously done this sort of thing before, as they started to talk amongst themselves about their past experiences.

It turned out that Mrs West had been married three times, each husband giving her a handsome settlement. Already, she seemed to be eyeing up various people seated.

She wanted to bring people together. Singles Club would be every Tuesday, with a big party night every fifth Saturday. Things started to bore me, I wished I hadn't bothered to turn up.

Mrs West continued, it was like listening to our old headmistress. Salsa classes were also on the menu, with Greek nights and poetry readings. A second half beckoned, so I decided I might leave. My mind struggled.

The bitter tasted good as I stood nervously at the bar, wondering *how* I was going to sit back down again without going bright red when all eyes focussed on me. At that moment I wished and beat myself up over the fact that I hadn't left after the first glass.

But then my life changed forever. Her voice came first, seductive. As I turned to look, my eyes absorbed her. Everything about her was perfect, even her name, Eveline Mangle.

Eveline Mangle was no ordinary woman, no, and that's a fact. She could speak three different languages and had an `A` level in History. But best of all she spoke to *me* first. "Can I join you in a glass of red?"

That was the beginning, the beginning of a long and fruitful relationship. After the initial stares and whispers, things settled down. Conversation seemed to flow and soon the event was over.

The cool air engulfed me and as Eveline spoke, I was even enchanted by the breath which exhaled at her every word. She gently touched my arm and said she couldn't wait until next time.

ΔΔΔ

Weeks passed, then a month. Our friendship blossomed and confidence grew. Eveline remarkably resembled a young Sarah Jane Smith, a former Dr Who companion. For me this was fantastic, as I was a keen Whovian.

It became even more fantastic, and surreal, when I received my first blow job. I couldn't believe it *and* in the ladies toilets too. I went to the gents, came out, Eveline grabbed me, smiled and then pulled me into the opposite room.

A lot of "strange" and exciting things happened after that. At the Singles Club to begin with and mostly in between group discussions.

Then things progressed.

I started to feel good about myself for once and so I should at nearly twenty. A change in diet, a little jogging and two stone gone just like that. Clothes changed too, along with a haircut and gel.

Eveline came for tea and mother seemed to like her. Although she did strip down to her underwear whilst mother washed up and only managed to fasten her blouse just as my only parent reappeared with tea and biscuits.

The Singles Club became extremely enjoyable. Drinks flowed along with good conversation. College became a pleasure and good results followed. I had a whole different outlook on life and I think people did towards me. Eveline Mangle worked at the local library and sometimes we`d meet there and have lunch at the adjacent café.

Two and a half months had passed and Eveline invited me to her flat. I knew what would happen, that`s why I`d postponed it for so long. I just wanted to be ready, feel good about myself, feel comfortable.

Sex for the first time, wow! And with Eveline. Everything was just perfect; drinks, a slow cigarette, a little jazz and all within the confines of her bohemian, one bedroom flat. Laughter, kisses and a little teasing, all led to the bedroom.

Candles flickered slowly and clothing was removed at the same pace. The pleasures of the female species were revealed between the sheets and they left me with a thirst for more.

How I loved life. Singing, whistling and posing in front of the mirror all became rituals within the bathroom. I had a fantastic sense of well-being and strutted to the bus stop each morning.

The Singles Club continued, bringing entertainment and good friendship from its members. Drinks were bought and drunk, jokes told and a few closer friendships formed between others. I owed so much to the Singles Club.

We were now very comfortable with each other. We`d invented silly words for each other, codes that only we could decipher. I also stayed at the flat at least a couple of nights each week.

Cooking had also become a big part of my life. It seemed to come as second nature to me; Indian, Chinese, Portuguese and a little African. The recipes came from books of course and were thoroughly enjoyed.

ΔΔΔ

June and the longest day approached. Christmas and the New Year were long gone. Warm weather greeted each morning and for the first time I actually felt good wearing T-shirts. A continuation with the diet, along with the jogging, had left me a slender eleven and half stone. Five stone lost!

My sexual appetite never seemed to be quenched, but was always satisfied by Eveline. She always found new ways to tease and never failed to excite.

It was a humid, cloudless Midsummer`s Day and Eveline wasn`t working. She`d asked me to come over from eleven onwards. We`d probably share a cigarette, then the bed, followed by a light lunch. Or that`s what I thought. The door was open, Nag Champa scented the air and the Viennese Waltz played on an old gramophone which was sat in the corner.

As I called out several times, my foot pushed open the bedroom door. There she stood, Eveline, dressed in a black, see through robe. Her voice sounded different when she spoke my name. As my hand touched her shoulder, the young Miss Mangle turned to face me.

A mixture of red and black swirled within her eyes. Her skin was paler, tinted with purple veins and sharp black talons stood proud on her finger ends. As the robe fell to the floor, not a single sound escaped me. She spoke and I listened.

"I`ve always loved this music, it brings back fond memories." With that she kissed me. I seemed to fall into a trance and then before long I lay naked on the bed. Wild, savage lust followed, like nothing I`d experienced before. Then we lay together, sharing a bottle of wine.

"What`s just happened to me?" It seemed a strange, but obvious question to ask.

"We *are* one now. We`ll never be apart."

"Never be apart? What do…what do…you…"

My body started to spasm and words faded to silence as I was unable to speak. I felt as if I was burning up inside. Writhing on the floor, new sensations rushed through my body, boiling through my veins. Talons grew on my hands and feet. My vision and sense of smell increased fifty fold. But the weirdest "thing" or "things" appeared on my back. Two wings! Two wings, I couldn`t believe it. They weren`t feathered like a birds, they were more like a pterodactyls.

Eveline flung open the windows leading to the veranda and I welcomed the slightly cooler night air. As if by instinct, my wings flapped and I took to the air. Rising above buildings and the fast paced world below, the adrenalin rush was like nothing I`d experienced before. A clear sky allowed for full vision as I soared higher and higher. Cars scurried below like rodents with torches and I could smell the various offerings of the takeaways. But I could also smell something else, the smell of humans. Each person had a different scent.

ΔΔΔ

It`s been a year since my first flight. Another Midsummer`s Day and another fine bottle of wine. The city looks great from up here, on the rooftop. Eveline will be home soon and I can`t wait.

My life, if that`s what you could call it, has changed forever. I suppose it would when you become a demon. It felt quite strange at first and a bit difficult to accept, but you soon get used to it.

You see, Eveline`s been around since the nineteen twenties. One night a master demon chose her, that`s what they do to keep the bloodline alive, choose females. After that the female has to travel the earth in search of her perfect partner. Some search for just days, others decades. You see it all depends on the scent of the human.

Then the female turns the chosen male into a demon. Apparently there are a lot of demons out there, but I`ve only met a few. I`m of the black winged variety and prefer to hunt at night. That`s what I have to do now, hunt. If the smell is delicious, then sadly we have to feast on the flesh. Ah, the scent of the feast!

I still like a good curry or fish and chips, but they don`t always agree with me now. Eveline always laughs when I`m in the loo and shouts "Told you so."

We can`t have babies, so it saves on condoms. But all that can change if a master is slain or just decides to die. You see when something like that happens, one of the couples will have a baby and we all move up the pecking order. Another downside is the constant moving and I don`t get to see mother that often. After a certain number of "feasts" and the fact that we don`t age, it`s time to "up sticks." Tonight should be most enjoyable, as Me and Eveline have encountered some very delectable people all week.

Who would have thought it? Me, the geeky fat boy, teased, ridiculed and destined to become one of life`s eternal virgins was destined to become a powerful demon; and all because I smelt just right. I`m so glad I didn`t smell bad.

And I`m so, *so* glad that Eveline waited until I`d slimmed down and looked this great. I couldn`t begin to understand how I`d feel if I had to spend my new, wonderful life looking like I did. But that`s just Eveline Mangle for you; loving, caring, thoughtful and kind. Life is full of surprises. You just never know what`s waiting around the corner and now, it`s a demon`s life for me.

It`s not a bad one. We get to travel, meet different people and I`ve managed to master the flying part. I suppose in some ways we`re doing the human race a favour, as the platter can be a gobby chav, an obnoxious drunk, the odd traffic warden or even politician.

I must apologise if you're a delightful breathing banquet. It`s just that your body has its own unique scent and a demon like myself will relish the feeling of devouring a helpless soul.

Nowadays, most people live to be seventy plus. I`ll probably live to be seven hundred plus! And it`s all down to the young woman I met. Eveline Mangle, demon in disguise, who decided to come along to the Singles Club.

Desert People –Part One

Each morning was the same, awake at five to the sound of the bell; calling to all from the watchtower on the west wall. Feet scurried, screams echoed down dark corridors as whips struck to hurry the pace and keys clanked at the guards` sides. The occasional "This one`s dead," uttered by one of the two syllable speaking officers, brightened up the day.

This was Kalakorn Prison; a one way sentence each time. No one had returned to civilian life or escaped within the last thirty years. There had been talk of one man`s success to freedom, but that was always considered folklore.

ΔΔΔ

Jal Serpeen, master thief and speaker of the dragon tongue rose to his feet, quickly standing by the iron bars which caged him. Reaching out to his left, the black haired man helped his cell mate stand alongside him.

"Hold tight old man, I`ll get you through the day." Jal`s gravel voice spoke. The old man nodded and half smiled.

He was near death, a week, a week and half at the most; but he hadn`t done badly for fifteen years hard labour. Simius Staple was his name and when the Reaper called to claim him, many secrets and wealth would accompany him.

Once a big name in Red City, he`d embezzled one too many money bags and ended up in Kalakorn. They couldn`t break him, most tried, so every now and then a "new" cell mate would be placed with him, in the hope of gathering information.

When he`d arrived, Jal was the perfect cell mate. The governors of the City expected the master thief to learn something and in turn *they* would learn something. That was the reason he was still alive. He`d received a savage beating on his arrival, but when you`ve lived and been to places like Jal Serpeen, a beating is just something you take. Three months had passed and maybe Serpeen only had a week or so to live.

The door slid to the right and the prisoner`s eyes did not meet those of the guards. They knew better. Two or three blows to the kidneys with a baton was the last thing you needed before starting work.

When the final iron gate lifted, not only did the light blind, but the air was hot and biting. Struggling to breath, holding your back, looking unfit for work, could all mean death. If you couldn`t work, you served no purpose. Salt or precious stones could not be mined in the desert, money would not be made and people would be unhappy.

What would it be today? Salt or stones? Left or right? Jal didn`t care it was all the same to him, just another day and he was alive.

"Bitch," he thought, "Yeh! Bitch." This referred to the woman who had put him here and he smiled at the very thought of her name.

It was right, to the salt mines. Crammed onto the wooden carts, the journey would take about an hour. No stops, just endless sand for the eye to view. After twelve hours work, the return journey would begin; then to the showers and feeding hall.

As workers piled into the carts, fighting broke out, guards swarmed and unconscious bodies were carried away.

"Settle down filth," Halg spoke. "Settle down filth, or I`ll be up all night watching you bastards hang." Halg Bleen, thief, murderer, soldier and now prison warden.

"Morning Jal," Bleen smiled. "Nice day to enjoy the sun."
No reply came, not even eye contact. Their paths had crossed before and animosity still loomed.

The barren desert offered little and the heat was already intense. Prisoners spoke very little, lost within their own personal thoughts. The party of convicts came to a halt, allowing gates to open so that the carts could roll through.

Instructions were not needed once inside, it was simple enough. On your feet, march down the tunnels and dig. Dig for the slabs of salt. Out they came, people cut them into various sizes and then they were then loaded on to different wooden carts.

Jal and Simius took the left tunnel. They`d worked it before. Most of the Salquar people also liked this tunnel and tended not to start fighting; unlike the more volatile of the prisoners, like the Kutché or Aldorian. Even though many of them hung, their numbers never seemed to dwindle.

Picks, shovels, hammers and barrows all worked with the hands of the condemned. The rhythmic beat of the sentenced continuously made money for the wealthy, while the guards looked on.

Serpeen worked twice as hard, doing enough for himself and the old man. Whatever he`d done, he deserved to die in peace, in his cell, not at the hands of these cruel bastards.

"Keep going old man."

"Yes, I am trying,"

"Break soon, a little fruit."

Staple`s eyes lit up at the thought and for half a dozen blows he matched pace with the master thief. But as the sixty year old man, whose end was near stumbled, Jal caught him as the gong sounded and the guards took no notice, as they too yearned for the mouth-watering fruit now on offer.

Fruit and water were given twice a day, along with a lunch of sultana bread and salted meats. The system allowed it. The "cattle" had to be fed well, otherwise it wouldn`t be productive. So at least you were well fed in Kalakorn, before your body was buried six foot under the very thing you`d mined.

Jal`s eyes and brain worked together, taking in the information. Deft fingers spoke, spoke the language of the deaf. Simius had worked with wealthy mutes, who were born this way and Serpeen had "done business" in the Calask Regions from which they hailed.

A joke was shared, but no lips moved. Jal took all in. A knee smashed into Simius`s back. Groaning, he lay face down. "On your feet cripple," the guard spoke. Smiling, he fingered his whip. "You`re slacking," the guard continued. "And you know what that means."

"Yes," Simius replied.

"Don`t answer back condemned," the large man kicked Staple`s ribs and a painful groan sounded. Condemned was their collective name and they all answered to it.

"Bring him." Two more guards moved, pulling Simius to his feet. Jal`s mind raced. What could he do? Standing helpless, nothing was the conclusion.

They`d take him away, hang him by his wrists for two hours and lash him a two dozen times. The heat would dry his throat, skin would burn in the sun, the strokes would not come all at once and salt would be applied to the welts.

A brutal punishment, that could break even the strongest and no one wanted second helpings. Something was wrong, Halg had ordered this, *he* must have gained knowledge about Simius and no longer needed him alive.

Two swift blows smashed into Serpeen`s guts. Falling to the floor he took a third to the back. "Make your move master thief, save the old man." As the guard spoke, he put the boot in. Jal protected his head, with arms and grunted as the footwear did the damage.

Shouts and screams suddenly echoed, the guards were being attacked. Some of the Aldorian had started to fight amongst themselves, eventually turning on one of the guards. These large, olive skinned men were wild and vicious. The unfortunate man lay face down in a pool blood, surely dead.

Arms and legs wind milled everywhere. Batons and whips joined the blows, whilst blood and teeth sprayed the floor.

Another cart drew into the scene. Two dozen men jumped to the ground, gathered and listened to a short command. The guards scattered, some dragging prisoners with them. Arrows whistled, striking and killing, then a second wave repeated. Eventually a handful of men stood, hands behind their heads, knowing their fate.

"Take those bastards away." Halg`s voice bellowed. "String that load of shite up, let the sun calm them down."

Ten men were loaded into one of the carts and slowly moved away. The remainder, half beaten by the guards were marched away. They`d be strung up on the high poles and left to bake in the sun. The lucky ones would hang at sunrise tomorrow.

In all the commotion, Jal, Simius and some of the Salquar had gone back to work. A good move, as prisoners were receiving beatings for nothing, just so the guards could vent their anger.

Tools sounded, the condemned worked and Jal and Simius had been forgotten for the time been. But a return to the cells would recall their fate. The day`s work ended and once again the prisoners moved in convoy across the empty desert.

Jal Serpeen closed his eyes and lost himself within his own thoughts. How did I end up in Kalakorn? I`ve been in and out of scrapes all my life. Nearly hung twice, been seconds away from losing my hands and my head. Some days I`ve had enough wealth to buy a Kingdom of my own and others I`ve barely had enough coppers to buy bread.

Serpeen spoke more words in his mind then laughed, because he knew the reason he was here, a woman; a beautiful, intelligent, wealthy woman, Rouska Bezai.

Rouska Bezai, she was all these things and more, she had been his lover on more than one occasion. Crossing paths as young thieves, the two had been enemies, then friends, partners and eventually shared a bed.

But the hypnotic, flame haired woman from the east had risen to power and position over the years. They`d had a business arrangement, with Serpeen taking most of the risks and only narrowly escaping death. But in the end, both had profited.

The last job had gone wrong, he`d walked into a trap after "acquiring" The Blue Sapphires of Elgoth. Half drugged with wine, the guards had taken him easily, Rouska never showed.

"All out," the guards spoke and Serpeen was ripped from his slumbered thoughts as the journey had come to an end. "Move it condemned, get showered." Feet shuffled, water sounded, clothes were discarded and prisoners soaked up the running pleasure along with soap.

Dried, clothed and combed, the men moved into the dining hall. Boiled fish, fresh bread, fruit and eggs flavoured the nostrils.

It wasn`t a bad meal, not for a prison and some looked forward to it all day, even though it rarely varied. But the "cattle" were fed well, they needed their strength and needed to work well in order to make money.

ΔΔΔ

Simius walked several paces in front, Jal entered the cell last, casting a quick glance before he did so. Guards paced up and down, locking prisoners in. Words were whispered when the two sat alone.

"You do not have long."

"I know."

"I will only live a week or so Jal, you know that."

Serpeen nodded and listened.

"When I am gone, you will soon follow. Master thief or not, you will not escape here."

"You think I don`t know that," Jal twiddled his thumbs.

"We have spoken and you have the information I have given you. I hope you are able to put it to good use."

"So do I Simius, so do I."

"I am a man of my word, if not always honest with money. But if it was not for you Jal Serpeen I would have been stabbed long ago."

Serpeen half smiled as he remembered his first day. Staple`s new cell mate had arrived just in time, as the old man was just about to get a blade buried within him. The new arrival had dispensed with them easily and no further trouble had come their way.

"Tell me young man."

Jal rolled his eyes sideways as Simius spoke.

"A personal question if I may. What was Rouska like. I mean you know, in the bedroom?"

Serpeen laughed, then coughed to stop himself chocking.

"Wilder, tougher and meaner than this place and worth all the risks."

Staple chuckled to himself. "I thought as much. When I was a young man I had an experience with a red haired woman."

"And what happened?"

"Well it is such a long time ago now. But she was quite a woman and I think you would say she was one hot bitch."

"One hot bitch?"

"Well maybe you would not say that, but I`ve listened to some of the other prisoners."

Smiling, Jal just stared at the old man.

"I am tired. We will talk more tomorrow, goodnight then."

"Goodnight." Jal turned closed his eyes and fell asleep, lost in his dreams.

The night passed quickly. Both cell mates were awake, resting with their own thoughts, waiting for the wakeup call. It soon came and as the two stood, one of the guards shoved his baton into Jal`s stomach.

"Morning Serpeen. How do you like that? Taste good eh?" As the black haired thief slowly rose to his feet, the baton struck his ribs. Jal cried out and clutched his side.

"A present thief," the guard, a young man, with green eyes pressed his face against Serpeen`s.

"Look at it in the tunnels." As he spoke, a small pouch was pushed into the prisoner`s tunic.

ΔΔΔ

The morning had moved slowly from the moment they turned left, left to the stone mines. The tunnels and shafts were cooler than those of the salt ones, but not as brightly lit. But one thought ached, burning through him, one puzzle, one mystery and it came in the form of a leather pouch.

"What the hell?"

Simius looked up as Jal spoke.

"Look at this." Serpeen rose to his feet, moved over to the old man and deftly placed the object into his hands.

Without attracting the attention of the guards, Staple glanced at the yellow stone marked with a red sun. "The mark of the desert people."

"Yes. But I thought they were only a myth."

"It seems not my young friend."

"Guards."

Jal moved swiftly, helping the older man to his feet and before the thick set guards reached them, the stone was cleverly hidden by the master thief.

Work and time dragged, like the heavy sacks of precious stones they moved to the carts. *Desert people, desert people?* The words became a question. Serpeen didn`t ponder too long. This was no time for a "good kicking" and if he daydreamed it just might come about. Simius could only take a couple of good blows and his heart would fail. So Jal needed to watch out for both of them.

ΔΔΔ

Shower, supper, cell. That was the order and Jal Serpeen sat in

38.

the third.

"What do you think?"

"I don`t know what to make of it. But it certainly means something."

"Do they *really* exist?"

"Again I cannot answer that question. You hear stories, tales, that sort of thing but I have never seen any definite proof."

Jal stood, paced then sat down again.

"Maybe the Salquar could help, but be careful who you speak with."

"Rouska."

"You don't think…"

"Maybe."

"But how could she…"

"She can be very persuasive"

"*Surely* she could not get anything in here?"

Serpeen raised his eyebrows, gesturing with his hands. No more conversation came, the two lay still until sleep consumed them. In the morning, the master thief woke early, unlike his cell mate. He would not work alongside Jal again, either in the salt or stone mines. He was dead.

Guards gathered, looking at Staple.

"What you done to him Serpeen?"

"Murderer. Don`t worry we`ll get the information we need." Questions came at him, but Jal did not reply.

Heavy footsteps sounded and Serpeen knew it was Halg.

"Old man finally dead then."

Jal nodded.

"Did well, I thought he`d of died long ago. His type always does. Easy life, money, never had it hard."

"He`ll be hard now, stiff `n` hard." Several guards laughed as the pathetic joke was made.

"What you do you think killed him Serpeen?" Halg stood in the cell now, alongside the breathing prisoner.

"Hard work I guess."

"Hard work? That lazy bastard never worked a day in his life. Just like the rest of you."

As the last word finished, several blows struck Serpeen and

down he went, holding his groin. Halg followed up with a kick and his victim groaned in agony.

"You're a thief Jal, not a bad one, but I knew your luck would run out one day; kept out of trouble in here too. But don`t try smart with me boy. NO ONE ever died from hard work in here."

Two guards pulled Serpeen to his feet and kept hold. Halg Bleen gave him three more blows to the midriff and a fourth to the jaw. "Better get to one of the carts, or I`ll deem you unfit." Halg spat the words, smiled and walked off.

Painfully, but as quickly as possible the beaten man moved, nearing the carts. If he managed to get on board, a little rest would come his way during the journey. Eventually his hand took the rail and he pulled himself up, taking the final place next to a tall tattooed man of the Salquar.

"Your friend is dead, news travels quickly. Do they know about the stone? Mmm, I think not, as you would not be alive Jal Serpeen. We shall work together you and I and decide what to do." As the deep, slow voice spoke, a hand flashed an identical stone to Jal`s. "Maybe we can escape." Serpeen nodded as the black skinned man named Malu spoke again.

ΔΔΔ

Bruised and still hurting, Jal worked the pick. Malu gathered the stones and hauled the full sack onto the wooden cart. They made a good team and several other sacks were filled before break.

"Who gave you the stone?"

"The young guard with the scarred neck."

"Did he say anything?"

"No. He gave me the stone whilst I walked back to my cells with the rest of the Salquar."

"Do you know anything about these desert people?" As Jal spoke, his body still ached and he wondered if another would come tonight.

"A little. They say they are a lost and ancient people, living in the desert wastelands."

Serpeen longed for more and after Malu had paused and pondered, which he often did, it came.

"They once lived in the towns and cities, like us. Good, honest, working people. But as the greed and corruption grew, they became fed up. The opulent and influential did not like the old ways; praying to the old gods, believing in magic and the spirit world. So they fled the towns and cities and made homes in the desert."

Another pause came and the captivated Serpeen quickly sucked an orange, relishing the taste.

"But the desert was not safe. Hunters were sent, to kill them, destroy them."

"Didn`t they fight back?"

"Sometimes. But many hunters came and *their* numbers became low. Eventually they vanished, never to be seen again. They live on in stories, dreams and myth."

"That`s quite a story. But I always thought they were just a myth."

"That`s what they want you to believe." As Malu spoke, he pointed in the direction of Red City. "*They,* control our lives. *They* tell you what to think and believe. Anything *they* don`t like or understand is destroyed."

"Do you believe in the desert people?"

"Yes Jal Serpeen, I do?"

"Why are you in here Malu?"

"For speaking, writing and teaching the old ways. My notes were burnt along with my home. But that was seven years ago."

"And what about family?"

"I sent them away, before I was arrested. I believe they are all safe, but I haven`t seen them in a long time."

"Seven years."

Malu nodded, both stood and the work started all over again. The usual routine was followed, along with the final leg, cells.

ΔΔΔ

"Serpeen, come here."

The master thief turned and moved towards the guard.

"Get some rest tonight. You`ll be starting an hour earlier in the morning."

"Why?"

"Don't get smart or you know what happens." A short baton prodded Jal as the guard spoke. "Be ready."

ΔΔΔ

As seven guards approached, Jal Serpeen stood waiting. No words were spoken, the door opened, footsteps sounded and the prisoner was marched away.

The man who had nearly sold the Blue Sapphires of Elgoth looked at the other passengers seated on the cart. Two Aldorian, a young man from Red City, Malu and a fifth Serpeen did not recognize. Not one of them spoke. The cart travelled east, through unfamiliar terrain. After about an hour they came to a halt. All jumped to the ground and just stood.

"Grab a shovel and follow me." One of the guards blasted an order. Words continued as he walked away.

"You men have been carefully selected to dig for a special prize, diamonds."

"*Diamonds?*" One of the Aldorian replied.

"That's right. Up there in the caves and we already have a buyer."

Jal's mind raced. What was all this about? Did they really have a buyer? Would they live?

The six men were soon at work, but all were thinking the same thing. Swiftly, the shovel struck, the guard went down and the two Aldorian men were upon him.

It didn't take long, neck snapped, he lay as lively as the sand. Shouts sounded, men scrambled like rabbits, now knowing which way to turn. Another guard fell, as the Aldorian rushed him. The rest of the officers were alerted by all the noise and commotion. Wasting no time, weapons were drawn.

Malu and Serpeen said it with a stare, let's start running before they kill us. And they were right.

The two Aldorian covered the ground quickly, putting distance between themselves and the rest. The man Jal Serpeen did not recognize stood, hoping the guards would leave him alone. He could not have been further from the truth. As several arrows thudded into his pigeon chest, a sword arced and took his head clean off. Now very few would recognize him.

"Move lad, come on." Jal encouraged the prisoner from Red City to keep up.

Gasping, he spoke with fear in his voice.

"I don`t want to die, I`m out in three months."

"You`re out now. Keep running, or you`ll end up like him."

As Serpeen spoke, the young man glanced back. Losing his nerve, panic set in, he began to cry. "No! No! Help me, I didn`t do anything."

"Leave him Malu." Jal shouted as the big, dark skinned man was about to help.

Eyes met. "He`s already dead." Breaking the stare, Malu listened to Serpeen`s words. Head down, arms pumping, he pounded at the sand with his legs.

The weak figure stumbled, fell and tumbled down the steep bank. Screaming, sand belching upwards as he continued in his three sixties, the swords finally claimed him, like blankets quenching a fire.

The pursuit ended. Two prisoners kept running, Serpeen and Malu; and the guards returned to the camp to gather their horses.

Sand, sand, sand, that`s all they could see. Legs hurt, burning, like the sun in the ever watching sky. Keep moving, keep running, don`t stop. That was the only thought on their minds. When the riders on horse-back came, the hunt wouldn`t last long.

Both slipped and the other helped. Sand tasted in their mouths and the barren wastes offered no haven for the escaped prisoners of Kalakorn.

As pain stabbed, lungs screamed for air, legs shouted stop and dune after dune challenged them. Would they escape? That`s what they hoped. But human legs would tire quicker than those of a horse and soon the guards would be upon them. Food and water were none along with shelter, time just ticked, waiting to play out the inevitable.

Malu glanced back, so did Serpeen, both looked at each other, both reached the same conclusion, no one pursues us.

"Where have they gone?"

Serpeen shook his head, slowed and began to walk. Malu moved

alongside and spoke.
"We must keep moving."
"And go where?"
"If we stop, we die."
"When the guards catch us, we die."
"Just keep moving my friend."

ΔΔΔ

Water slowly trickled, tasting like a fine wine, quenching thirst and both men would have given anything for more. The cluster of rocks offered shade from the relentless sun and Malu was satisfied that he had found the small plant, whose roots contained the valuable liquid.

Dusk and new sounds came to life. Still no hunters on horseback and the air became cooler, more breathable. The two "free" men decided to rest and sleep, but both knew what the morning would bring.

ΔΔΔ

"Good work men, good work." Halg Bleen smiled as he looked at the dead two bodies. "And where are the other two?"
"They approach now, on the cart." As he spoke, the guard pointed.
Bleen laughed. "Only Serpeen and the black man left."
"Burn these bodies. Ready my horse and we`ll hunt at dawn"

ΔΔΔ

"We must move Jal."
The thief rose to his feet gathering himself. Nodding, he spoke.
"Lead the way."
A steady pace was set, the two spoke, enjoying jokes and tales. Both kept moving, hoping for a miracle, but expecting the worst.

But soon hooves, laughter and a familiar voice, all came in one mixture.
"Run!" Malu did not reply, he just obeyed.
"That`s right Serpeen, keep running, but death`s coming old friend."
Bleen`s voice bellowed over the dunes, as he approached with six other riders.

The chase was on, two men against seven, who rode on horseback. They didn`t charge them, outrun them, overtake them. Just

44.

behind, but always there, the riders teased; on and on, legs carried, slowing, tiring. Each glance back brought the vision of silhouetted hunters.

"Malu!" Serpeen screamed as his friend disappeared. Engulfed by the sand within seconds, only his upper body remained. Seconds passed, Jal stared, Malu shook his head, smiled, then vanished.

"One down, one to go." Laughter filled with hate followed, as Bleen shouted his words.

Several hours passed. A human body can only take so much. When all strength has drained, emotions, determination and a will to survive all kick in, but even these are eventually sucked from the very soul.

Why don't they just kill me? This was the last thought that entered Jal Serpeen's mind. The sand dune loomed and he pathetically started to ascend, falling twice, like a tavern drunk at midnight.

Four feet, three, two, the peak drew nearer and came. Blurred vision brought a scattering of branches and stump that was once a mighty tree.

Slumping he fell to the dry wood. Motionless, only his eyes flickered. Hot skin sweated under the sun, dry lips tasted beads of salty liquid and more stung his eyes as they struggled to view.

Purple robes lightly billowed, bare feet walked the sand and blue beads adorned the ankles. The face was covered, but the thief knew it was a woman who approached. The graceful movements and hands revealed all.

Drawing nearer, the robes revealed more flesh beneath. Light brown skin, curvaceous, covered with jewellery and several tattoos. A face came within inches of his own; warm, seductive brown eyes stared out from behind the veil.

A petite hand removed the veil to reveal a young, attractive face. Soft lips moved, showing perfect white teeth and the words flowed soothingly.

"You're safe now Jal Serpeen. We shall take care of you." It was like a beautiful song when she spoke, a hand touched his face and Jal passed out.

45.

Breathing was easy and calm. The bed was soft, silk sheets felt good against his skin and aches and pains seemed to flow out of his resting body. Unfamiliar scents surrounded him, along with voices. This was paradise.

Jal`s eyes opened, varying colours of rugs hung from the walls, green copper vessels housed burning incense and a bowl of fruit sat alone on a wooden table. Sitting up, he realized he was inside a large tent of some kind.

The tent flap opened, an older woman appeared, took one look and vanished. Moments later, the woman from the desert stood outside staring in.

"Good, you are awake." As she spoke, she moved into the tent and Jal was pleased with the view. A purple skirt, split up the middle, revealed shapely legs. Her hair was tied back, breasts were just covered with the same fabric and moons and other symbols were tattooed onto her midriff.

Serpeen started to rise from his place of rest, realized he was naked and remained slightly embarrassed under the sheets.

"I shall fetch you some new clothes when you have washed." She smiled teasingly. "You have something to hide under there?" Her eyebrows rose in question.

"No."

"Mmm, a thief with nothing to hide?"

Serpeen did not reply.

"Please, take a bath," she motioned with her hands.

Standing on his feet, the sheet fell away and Jal stood naked. Eyes met and the young woman let the tiniest smile escape, whilst briefly casting a glance up and down.

"This way." Serpeen walked in the direction her hand pointed. Following, the younger female looked at the older woman standing silent. Both giggled as the thief stepped outside and they both glimpsed at his behind.

More tents were scattered outside, people moved here and there. A larger, red tent contained the wooden constructed bath. Hot water soothed his body, taking away the aches and pains. Green and blue soap was available to wash away the sand and grime of the desert.

The woman who had come to him in the desert gently massaged his shoulders and neck, then washed the thief's back. The arousing sensation stopped, rising, she undressed and joined him in the water and both washed together.

Five minutes passed and an older man entered the tent.

"Is this him Sori?"

"Yes father."

"Join me in my tent when you have bathed."

Then he turned and left.

Sori rose and left, wrapping towels around her. Two women entered, leaving towels and clothing for Serpeen.

The black sandals and trousers fit well, feeling comfortable. A green silk shirt was a welcome change to that of the prison attire and he quite liked the stylish black waistcoat with silver patterns woven within the fabris.

Grapes, apples, oranges, bananas and many other fruits sat on plates. Others housed dates, cheeses and fish. Wine waited to be poured and happy people, deep within conversations, all looked pleased to see him.

Sori sat with her father and motioned for him to join them.

"Welcome Mr Serpeen," the father spoke. "Please enjoy and relax." A goblet appeared and was soon filled. Several plates of food were brought before him, smelling delicious.

Music began, filling the tent, as wooden and string instruments were played. Three young women started to dance and were in turn joined by males.

"Ah! This is the life paradise."

"You approve Jal Serpeen?" Sori gestured with her hand as she spoke. The master thief nodded and gulped down more wine. Smiling, showing all teeth, he spoke.

"Yes, I approve. Certainly better than where I've been spending my time lately."

ΔΔΔ

Horses galloped, closing in. Hooves left prints, causing small scatterings of sand. One rider came within inches, just enough to catch the body with his knee. It fell to the side, face up in the dunes.

"It`s him!"

"It`s him alright, who else would it be?" Bleen stole the conversation and the guard became silent.

"Not so tough now, are we Serpeen?"

Halg Bleen dismounted. Moving over to the body, he kicked the corpse.

"Shame I didn`t kill you myself, but never mind, the desert`s done the job."

Laughing, Bleen fell to his knees and grabbed the dead man`s hair, lifting the head off the sand.

"Too bad *Mr Master Thief*, too bad," he whispered in to a deaf ear, "Feels better to be alive." More laughter came and he slapped Serpeen`s cheek with a spare palm. "Feels better to be alive."

Halg stood and pointed. "You, get that shite of the sand and onto your horse. We`ll burn him back at the prison, for ALL to see."

"What`s that?"

"What`s what?"

"That there?"

"Looks like a scarf or something."

"A scarf?"

"Yeh, a scarf, or veil, whatever they`re called."

"What would he want with a scarf?"

"A veil?"

"Whatever. What would he want one for?"

"Don`t know."

As the two men swung the corpse over the horse, one walked over to the branch. His hand reached down and grabbed the trapped fabric. Holding it before his eyes for several seconds, the prison guard unfurled his fingers and released his find. Gently falling to the ground, the purple veil blew away, like a lost sail on an endless sea of sand.

48.

For Sale

Voices. That`s all I hear, voices. Calling out, whispering, suggesting, asking, teasing. Haunting my mind, twisting my thoughts, draining my sanity, this cacophony of icy menacing sounds invades when I should be resting; resting peacefully within the sheets, charging my batteries for the next day to come.

Shadows. That`s all I see. They too call when the sun leaves and darkness is cast and allowed to play.

Shapes form from the blackness. Twisted, hideous faces, distort into indescribable contortions. Black, emotionless eyes stare. Bottomless wells of foulness glare and burn into my very soul.

So here I am again, tired and just wanting sleep. One night`s sleep, that`s all I ask. Please, I need to rest, awake and enjoy my life.

My life? My life was good, until last September. That`s when I was promoted and also earned a fat, juicy bonus. Easy money in the "big smoke", new car and a trip to the countryside to find our dream home. Seems such a long time ago now, but I remember how it all began.

The "For Sale" sign almost jumped out and sat alongside me in the passenger seat. I had to stop and take in the view.

The iron gate sitting within the stone wall looked perfect, although it did need painting. Stone slates were buttered with a light spread of moss, and chimney pots longed to exhale smoke once more. Leaded windows kept secrets I longed to know. Worn mullions were furnished with ivy and a proud oak tree stood guarding the west gable.

Beckoning, calling, drawing me nearer, the wooden door invited as I strode up the stone path. What delights waited inside? Open fires, beams, a cellar awaiting vintage wine, an Aga and much more. It was the house Trudie *would* love. It was the house where she could host parties, it was the house of our dreams.

I wished at that moment she were at my side. But that`s the down side of business, the downside of the "professional couple." I was here, on home soil, holding the fort and she was away clinching a deal in New York.

Hand and door almost connected, as I just had to touch and try the knocker. But there he stood, Mr Tackler, right at my side.

Within minutes we were chatting away, laughing and joking. After admiring the car, Lamborghini Reventon, Mr Tackler asked me to follow him to his office to collect the keys.

The two mile journey seemed like twenty, as his Renault Clio maintained a steady twenty eight miles per hour.

Parking was easy, other vehicles were scarce and the high street seemed half asleep.

As I expected, the whole exterior and interior of the estate agents were both dated by thirty years. Didn`t this man know it was the twenty first century? Even the telephone was an unheard of yellow. Not much conversation came and soon I had the keys.

"Go! Go," he said.
"Take as much time as you like. I`ll be here when you`re done."

Those were the only words Mr Tackler spoke. Without wasting any time, I sped back to the house in a third of the time.

Breathless, trembling, I turned the key. Heart pumping, I felt like a child with a rush of excitement before his birthday. The heavy door belched open, accompanied with the cliché creak.

Sunlight entered, along with myself. Dust speckled the air and an unfamiliar scent lingered. Everything met expectations and as I explored, nothing was less than satisfying.

The stone fireplace stood proud, along with several pictures. French windows divided myself and the classic English garden. Wooden and stone floors ran throughout the downstairs. A wry smile escaped as I entered the kitchen and the small snug longed for a comfy chair.

As I transcended between floors, the oak staircase mesmerised me. Both bathrooms were pure relaxation, only missing lit candles. And the master bedroom, housing a magnificent four poster bed, just lacked Trudi.

That was it! *Nothing* would change my mind. I had to buy this house. Locking the door behind me, struggling to breathe, I raced to my car.

"A pleasure doing business with you young man."
As Mr Tackler spoke, a satisfied gleam spread across his face. His hands rubbed together, then through his hair.

He'd accepted my offer, said he'd contact the bank first thing Monday and sort things out. He trusted me, told me I was the right person for the house. Of all the business deals I'd had anything to do with, I'd never experienced anything like this.

In fact all of my previous business deals had involved hours of conversation and masses of paperwork. But before the boring part, clients were dined at the finest restaurants, sampled the finest wines, attended the West End shows and enjoyed the sights of the capital.

But that's what people expect when they're willing to invest vast sums of their hard earned money with you.

A few weeks passed, paperwork was completed and I travelled between London and the country.

Texts and emails were exchanged, as Trudie was staying on in New York. That didn't matter, it gave me time to get the house in some sort of order and we'd have the perfect Christmas together.

I began to work from home more and more, occasionally phoning the office. Late nights in front of the fire became a must, along with a whiskey. Menacingly, that's when it all started.

The house became cold, regardless of heating, doors occasionally jammed, shadows seemed to follow me and a constant presence watched as I lay beneath the sheets.

As regular as clockwork, Tackler would drive past. Slowing down as he reached the house, he'd stare from the vehicle, then continue down the lane.

Something watched me, some cold malevolent being, whose name or like I did not know. The one became two and it became apparent that about eight or nine of them were ever present. I knew by the way the shadows moved, the voices, the way they controlled me in different ways.

The first one slammed doors, moved objects and occasionally danced across the walls in a shadowy human form. Things became worse. Cold water suddenly scalded me, food went stale overnight and welt marks appeared on my body, as if I had been beaten during the night. Weeks passed.

ΔΔΔ

New horrors have arrived. Only certain rooms are accessible. Ablutions are permitted, but the shower burns after several minutes, signalling my time is up. Gifts rot on the back seat of my car, which is jailed within the garage. What welcome will Trudi receive when she returns to England?

I anticipate banishment from the kitchen, as I am now confined to the bedroom and bathroom. The twenty four pack of assorted crisps and packet of chocolate biscuits, which I managed to smuggle back, are running low.

My body is weak and the journey to the bathroom difficult. Confined to my bed, I can see the cars as they pass by outside.

What evil dwells within this house? What secret is unknown to the rest of the world, hidden, only known to the locals? They too walk past, stop, glance knowingly up at the bedroom window, then go about their daily business.

The sign went up like a menu. Tackler was the head waiter, welcoming, pleasant, taking my order. But *I* was the dish, served up to feed this ever hungry stomach of evil and hate. How many more courses had it devoured? How many more innocent victims had suffered the same fate that would come my way within the next twenty four hours?

I'm too weak to do anything now, even the pen is too heavy, so my thoughts replace words. They'll probably find my diary, but then again maybe they won't. Maybe the next buyer will fall lucky and find it, read it and tell of this village's foul secret.

As my eyes gaze out from beyond my cell, the faces and voices have returned. Dancing across the walls, the grotesque images invite me to join them. I wish death would relieve me of my increasing madness.

I've never been a religious man, but if there is a God maybe he'll reunite me in heaven with Trudi if she suffers the same fate.

A large, bearded man is outside, waiting in a green van. Tackler's pulled up alongside him and they're sharing words.

The two are standing, staring up at the window. Tackler's hands

52.

are rubbing together; another plate of flesh, bone and soul will quench the diners' cravings and that smile is back on his face, as the bearded man opens his van doors.

At each blow the sound of the hammer thunders through my mind and the distorted faces accompany with shrills of twisted laughter. The sign has been erected and once more the house is "For Sale".

The Beggar

Prologue

We are all born the same, live our lives and eventually die. Life unfolds, revealing many things; some men prosper whilst other fail, wealth and poverty are divided amongst us all. People aspire to be wealthy, acquire materialistic items and rise above their neighbours.

Intelligence cannot be bought. Success should not be measured by one`s wealth, fine clothes or house in which they live.

Society is what society breeds. A food chain is created, people fighting each other to reach the top. Offspring follow in the footsteps of their teachers and so gold, silver and sapphires become more precious than water, bread and shoes.

The sun and moon are never thought of, the tides ebb and flow unnoticed and the know how to create wealth becomes greater than the know how to create fire.

Is there really a god? Does an all-powerful being or beings watch over us? Are we punished in the next life for the lives we have led in this one?

What happens when a civilisation reaches a state of wealth beyond our wildest dreams? Others work, while the rich lay idle. Water comes from the tap, fruit and vegetables are grown for someone else to pick and the most succulent dishes should be served on the finest gold platters.

ΔΔΔ

"Which one do you want?"

"All of them."

No laughter followed, the woman just gestured to the shop keeper and he came running.

"Yes madam, of course madam. A wise choice madam, shall I wrap them for you?"

"Yes."

As she spoke, the woman walked away, looking rather disdainfully and began to filter through bottles of perfume with a pale hand.

The couple exited the shop. Making eye contact with another husband and wife, they proceeded to an eating house. Polite conversation was made, the four were seated outside by a large man with greedy eyes and menus were soon brought.

ΔΔΔ

"Come along Clarissa."

"Why *should* I have to walk?"

"It`s a lovely day. It`s nice to walk."

"A carriage would have been quicker."

"We can take a carriage home darling." A third voice spoke from behind the mother and daughter

"Thank you father."

The blonde haired, eleven year old let go of her mother`s hand and held her father`s. Smiling she spoke again. "Could I have a new necklace to go with my new dress?"

"I don`t see why not sweetheart."

The mother turned to look, but the father spoke again. "And I think it`s about time *you* had some new jewellery. Say about two thousand, maybe three. That nice bracelet you like, the gold one." Smiling, they all shared a hug. "Business is good, so let`s enjoy the rewards."

ΔΔΔ

Four younger pairs of legs followed the older pair. One boy pretended to walk with a limp, another had removed his shoes. Howls of laughter accompanied them, along with abuse.

"What is it?"

"What are you," another spoke.

"He`s a pig."

"An animal of some sort?"

"Are you from beyond the mountains? They say the towns and cities there are dirty and that the people are savages and unintelligent."

"He`s a savage then."

"Can you speak?" No reply came.

"He can`t speak, he can`t speak."

Various animal imitations followed, a dog, a cow, a wolf. Small stones were thrown at the man`s back. He didn`t turn to scold the young boys, he didn`t run, instead he just kept walking, travelling further into the town.

His tormentors had first sighted him by the river, to the east of the town, the town of Sorbil. This was a very wealthy town, rich in vineyards, precious stones and silk.

Following him for over twenty minutes, he had moved away from the river and now approached the main street, which would eventually take him into the square for all to see.

More eyes had now sighted this "thing." Tongues wagged and fingers pointed. One of the boys had been pulled away by his mother. A group of men had now gathered and also followed.

"Tell the Mayor."

"We can`t, he`s away."

"Where?"

"On holiday."

"Oh!"

Bare, filthy, bruised feet eventually stood still. Worn, tattered clothes hung from him and thick matted hair sat on top of a weary head. Longing eyes gazed and he eventually sat on the cobbled street.

No one spoke to him or approached. His original pursuers had all gone, but many eyes still viewed. Dirty hands held a wooden bowl as he looked up in hope.

"So what do we do?"

"What is it?"

"I think it`s a man."

"No! No man would look like that."

"It`s a beast."

"If it`s a beast, what shall we do with it?"

"Wait until the Mayor returns."

"When will he return?"

"The day after tomorrow."

"Where`s he gone."

"To the Southlands, on holiday."

"Yes that`s right. He`s not been Mayor long has he?"

"No, only six months."

"That's right. We lost the old Mayor quite suddenly and he was elected."

"Shame, I like the old Mayor."

And so the three men continued to converse between themselves; the Banker, the Diamond Merchant and the Vineyard Owner. A fourth man walked towards them and all seemed pleased to see him.

"The Judge, the Judge is here."

"He'll know what to do."

"Look, look at that. What shall we do?"

These last words were directed at the tall thin man, who looked like an eagle.

"Now gentlemen, let's keep calm. We can't do anything rash or stupid. I know *what* we should do, but we shall have to wait until the Mayor returns."

"But you're the Judge."

"We must wait until the Mayor returns."

"That's right. That's why we elected him."

"The Mayor will decide and we shall help him."

"And then the Judge will pass sentence."

"That's correct I will."

"So we'll just have to wait."

"I suppose so."

"It doesn't look dangerous."

"No it doesn't."

"We'll just keep away."

"Continue as normal."

"What will the people say?"

"We'll just have to wait and see."

"I wish the Mayor was here now."

"So do I."

"He'll be back soon."

ΔΔΔ

Hours passed, people stared, keeping their distance but still curious. Not speaking, the half-starved man just sat, longing for food, water or even conversation. Noses were held as townsfolk passed, one woman nearly fainted and another had to rush into a local tavern to be sick.

"Pig! You pig."

"Clarissa, come here."

Ignoring her parent`s orders, the girl ran towards the man. Brandishing a riding crop, the spoilt young female began to beat him. "You filthy pig. Horrid thing! Go! Leave our nice town, leave us alone savage pig."

Hands covered his head, as the man of about fifty suffered at the hands of the eleven year old. The father grabbed her, stopping the punishment. He took the riding crop in his own hands, throwing it to the ground in disgust.

"Uh! It`s all dirty. Quickly, a carriage, you need a bath and fresh clothes."

"Yes, come along darling," the mother added to what her husband had said. "We`ll buy you some new clothes and a new riding crop."

As the family left, others laughed in approval, whilst some smiled and applauded. But amid all the commotion and fuss, a newcomer to the town had arrived. No one heard the hooves of his horse, as he entered the square, saw him dismount and take a table outside where he ordered one of the finest wines the town had to offer.

"Yes sir, an excellent choice." The man serving absorbed the beautiful red and black cloth the stranger wore, his fine, pointed leather boots, well-manicured hands and clean shaven face. And he couldn`t help but noticed the black, stovepipe hat that the man had removed.

Smiling, nodding, taking the food order, he glanced again and for a moment stood perplexed. No! It cannot be. Looking again, he confirmed the stranger`s eyes were blue and not brown, as he thought they had been when he first arrived.

"Shall I arrange for your horse to be taken to the stables sir?"

"Yes. That would be most kind, thank you."

The food was brought to his table and he spoke again.

"I shall be staying for two nights and be leaving at noon on the third

day. Where would you recommend I stay?"
"Oh that's easy sir. Over the road," he pointed. "The hotel offers

excellent accommodation and a nice light breakfast."

"Is this place expensive?" As the stranger spoke again, his voice was smooth and strong, each syllable was pronounced perfectly. The question took the other man by surprise and he stuttered at the beginning of his sentence.

"Eeexp... expensive? Yes sir, it's the most expensive in town, but has an excellent reputation. If you don't mind me saying sir, you look like a man who can afford expensive things in life."
"Of course I can." He smiled after he had spoken, clasped his hands, closed his eyes and took in a deep breath, "Smells delicious."

Sipping his wine, the stranger ate the small manageable pieces he had cut. He paid, leaving a handsome tip, stood and made his way towards the hotel.

Afternoon came and people went about their business. Horses, some with carriages, passed, people passed and still the man in rags just sat in the square. He fell asleep twice, longed to make eye contact and held his bowl up in hope of food.

He was avoided like dog foul, a disease no one wanted, a "thing" that didn't "fit in" with the town. Night called, bringing a chill, along with a cat out for a prowl and hunt. The feline wound teasingly towards him, shoved it's nose into his face, then turned and left.

ΔΔΔ

"Morning. I will have the eggs and some of the wonderful coffee from the Blacklands."
"Thank you sir."

The young woman took the order and left, leaving the well-dressed stranger to his own company. Other people in the dining room cast quick glances and conversation was whispered about him.

Rising from his chair, he politely nodded and left. Standing outside, he casually lit a cigar, inhaled, waited, then exhaled. Confidently, he walked across the road towards the place where he had eaten yesterday.

"Morning sir."

"Morning. I would like to dine here again, same table, same time."

"Of course sir," Half smiling, the tavern owner moved closer and spoke again.

"I wondered sir could I ask you a question?"

"Certainly."

"Mmm, have you seen anything like that before? And do you know what it is?"

"Two questions."

"Two questions?"

"Never mind," The stranger knowingly smiled and continued. "I am teasing you, I apologise. Yes, he is a beggar."

"A beggar?"

"A beggar. Yes. And he looks hungry."

"Hungry?"

"Hungry. Do you have any food for him?"

"Food for *him*? But I don`t think he has any money."

"The man is half starved. Surely you can spare a little food and wine."

"If he can`t pay for it, he can`t have it."

"Show him some kindness. Help him."

"Is that what you do with beggars?"

"It is what you do with anyone who is in need of help. At this moment in time, he is not as fortunate as you."

"I`ll have to think about it. Talk with my friends."

"He may be dead by then."

The other did not reply and the well-spoken man bid him good day and left. Walking across the square, the elegant stranger passed the beggar. Eyes met and for a moment the ragged man thought he recognized him. Nothing was said.

ΔΔΔ

"Can you imagine, giving him food."

"It`s disgusting."

"It should be arrested and run out of the town."

"And it`s called a beggar."

"Morning ladies," the newcomer interrupted the conversation and the two ladies turned to look at him. One blushed, whilst the other spoke.

"Ah! Good day sir. We were just saying it`s disgusting having that thing out there."

"There are many disgusting things in this world, but a starving man in need of help is not one of them."

"And have you seen one of these beggars before?"

"Yes madam, I have."

"Where, where have you seen one? And what is your name sir?"

"I have travelled to many different lands and have seen many different people starving and in need of help. Names vary, but beggar will suffice here."

"And *your* name?"

"Over time, I have had many names. Most just call me Rider now."

"Rider, what sort of name is that?"

"It is my name." Saying no more, he smiled, turned and left.

ΔΔΔ

Soon more people were talking, discussing. Who is this Rider? What is a beggar? They were perplexed and confused.

Another day had nearly passed. The beggar was tired and weak. Still food and water were none. No one came to him, except the cat. Remarks and repulsion stayed with him, along with the pain in his stomach called hunger.

ΔΔΔ

"Another glass of wine sir?"

"No thank you. It is a nice evening for a walk, before I retire."

The tavern owner smiled and Rider continued. "Again, I would like to eat lunch here, noon if possible."

"Certainly."

"I am expecting company, a business associate."

"Thank you sir. A table for two then." The owner spoke, as Rider stood and left.

ΔΔΔ

A little cloud drifted across the sky, the sun brought some warmth and people walked here and there, some quickly, others with all the time in the world.

"The breakfast was delightful."

"Thank you sir." the young woman shyly replied to the immaculately dressed newcomer.

"I shall freshen up in my room and then I would like to settle my account."

"Yes sir."

"Could you send a message to the stables?"

"Certainly, I`ll go myself."

"Thank you. Would you tell them to keep my horse inside and I shall collect him at three."

"At three sir, I`ll tell them."

"That is very kind of you."

Taking a pocket watch from his waistcoat, Rider checked the time. His hand took hold of his leather bag and expensive leather boots started to walk. He looked very much the Victorian gent.

People spoke within their own company as he strode across the square. He knew, eyes took all in, he knew they talked about him, knew they didn`t agree with him. A young boy, about ten, almost bumped into him.

"Sorry young man." Rider spoke and held out a reassuring hand. The boy returned a scathing look for one so young. Pulling away, he found his parents.

"That`s him mother. Rider they call him, the one who tells us to feed the beggar."

"I know darling."

"Come along you two, let`s go." The father spoke to both of them.

Rider ran an index finger across his lips, half smiling. "Mmm," escaped his mouth as he watched them stroll away.

As the hours passed, events repeated themselves. Townsfolk whispered, spoke behind his back. Some questioned him abruptly, asking why they should help the beggar, feed him, *pay* for him. Totally absurd most thought. They had money, wealth and status. Each of them had worked hard, saved and were able to enjoy the better things in life.

ΔΔΔ

A cool breeze blew through the town and people went about

their business as Rider approached the tavern. The owner smiled and showed him to his table.

"Wine please, red, make it Merlot."

"Of course sir."

"Two glasses."

A young man brought the glasses, wine and a menu. "No need for the menu. The chicken and the lamb will suffice, vegetables and roast potatoes."

"Anything else sir?"

"No, that will be all. My friend will be here soon."

"Thank you sir." The waiter left and Rider enjoyed a glass of wine.

The meal was ready and three came to serve, including the owner who spoke.

"Your friend is late sir. Would you like to wait a little longer?"

"No, no I do not wish to wait. My friend is here now."

"Where sir?" The owner spoke, looking at the same time.

"There, he approaches now." Rider pointed.

"Where, where…" His words were cut short as he saw who walked towards them.

Slowly, painfully, trying to resist, the beggar drew nearer. *That`s right beggar, come and join me.* These words were strong in his mind and he could not refuse.

"But he can`t eat here."

"He can and he will." Eyes met and Rider held his gaze.

"I asked you yesterday if I could dine here with a friend. You said yes and here he is." The beggar now stood by the table.

"But not him, you never said…"

"Silence! You, pour him some wine." A glance and a pointed finger prompted one of the waiters.

"I must…"

"SILENCE!" The owner stopped instantly, words caught in his throat.

"Sit down beggar," Rider gestured with a hand, speaking dismissively.

A trembling hand reached for the wine. "That`s right beggar help yourself."

The man in rags gulped, spilling down his front.

"Pour him some more, then leave us."

Without hesitation his glass was full, but the owner spoke once more.

"Sir, Rider, I must protest. This is my business and I…"

"I will not tell you again." The voice was menacing and slow.

"You will NOT speak to me again," his voice withered the protestor and continued.

"You will leave us to enjoy our meal. And you shall reflect on your very being, your life as a man, a human. You do not possess any compassion, show any thought or kindness to someone in need. What are you?" The speaker shook his head, eyes changed from blue to brown to black and the listener stood white with fear.

"I wish to speak to you no more. GO! And let us enjoy this food and wine. What kind of town this is? What kind of people does it house? Look, look at the sky and pray. Now go."

Clouds gathered overhead, grey and thick. An icy wind blew and silence fell across the town; not a single bird could be heard.

"What did he mean, what`s happening?" The young waitress had fear in her voice.

"Quickly, everyone leave them." Ushering all his staff away, the owner looked back at the two men seated and then at the sky.

"What shall we do?" Another young voice sounded.

"The Mayor isn`t back yet."

"Let`s find the Judge." All were speaking now, all asking questions, voicing opinions, but getting nowhere.

"Ah beggar! Beggar, beggar, beggar. How are you?" A pause followed.

"Not speaking to me?" Another pause.

"That is a shame, after I have gone to all this trouble." Rider motioned with a hand across the table. "The lamb is excellent. Please, try some." A slice was carved and placed on the beggar`s plate.

Grey clouds were been replaced by black, rain loomed and the wind started to howl. Some townsfolk just stared at the sky, others ran for cover. A black furred feline quickly dashed across the street, finding shelter under the tavern table.

"Mr Sativola, there you are." The cat mewed. "Yes I know, you do not like the weather."

Rider reached down, picking up the worried animal. Deftly opening his bag with a spare hand, he popped the cat inside and it seemed content.

"Now beggar, where were we?" The starving man ate, whilst gulping wine between mouthfuls. His body was filled with welcoming sensations as the meal progressed.

"Slow down, digest your food."

One of the nearby tables suddenly took flight, hurtling passed their heads. Two chairs followed. A couple held on to each other as the wind overpowered them. Both were taken along the cobbles on their backs. The beggar`s eyes looked on in panic.

"Alright beggar, you can speak." Rider`s eyes flashed and speech came to the man in rags.

"Save them, please save them. Please stop." His voice was full of emotion and belonged to an educated man.

"You know I cannot do that. We had a deal. Remember?"

"You must. I`ll do anything, take me instead."

"How many times have we been over the rules?"

"But…"

"No beggar. You have had your chance."

"I`m not a beggar!"

Rider laughed and shook his head. "You are. You are a beggar."

"No, I`m the …"

"You are no longer the Mayor. You have a new position now and have been renamed by myself."

"These are my people."

"Your people? They were never your people. If they were, then they would have helped you."

"They didn`t recognize me."

"*Exactly* beggar, that is the point. Oh! Watch this beggar."

Rider broke off the conversation. He stood to get a better view, as rain began to pour. A small fat man was lifted off his feet and smashed into a wall by the savage wind.

Lying broken and face down, the downpour washed away the blood trickling from his head. Several more bodies suffered in the same way. Cobbles exploded, causing a woman to lose her head and the hotel burst into flames. Screams echoed through the town, people ran in uncontrollable panic and others collapsed in sudden fear.

"Eat up beggar, the meat will be cold."

"I beg you please."

"YOU SEE, you *are* a beggar. You are begging for me to stop."

"Why?" The beggar began to cry.

"Let us remind ourselves old friend." As he spoke, Rider took a sip of wine.

"I`ll never be your friend."

"Alright, new partner then. You were once the Mayor of this town, this foul town full of foul people. But it goes further back than that beggar. Does it not?"

"Yes."

"Yes it does, it goes a long way back."

Eyes flickered different colours and a hand passed over the table. A red mist appeared in the wood, eventually becoming a mirror. Blurred images swirled into focus and words were spoken. "Take a long look beggar. Look and know why.

The town stood, but as a small village, almost three generations ago. A lake was drained, making way for new housing. Small tribes suffered, losing their way of life, but others gained in wealth. Trees were cut, affecting wildlife and humans who lived within the woodland. Rich people came, buying land and property and the town flourished.

An ancient and peaceful people, living to the south, were slaughtered by "hired men", just so business men from the cities could come and hunt "peacefully" in the holidays. All the old ways died out, children starved, because their parents could not afford the new high standards of life.

Offspring followed in their parent's footsteps, sibling sometimes killing sibling, just to gain wealth and power. On the surface, all was clean and innocent, an expanding town, thriving with entrepreneurs and wealth. But underneath, it reeked with deceit and death.

Murders took place, amongst friends and family; some so that young mistresses could be wed, others to allow someone else to wear the robes of power.

The beggar saw himself. Blood on his hands, he stood over his predecessor clutching a knife. Then his first wife lay dead in the stables after he had poisoned her.

"You murdered her beggar to marry this one." Rider broke the silence and the visions continued.

A beautiful woman stood at the beggar's side. But he was smartly dressed and commanded respect, he was the Mayor. *She* was his new bride. Laughing, they shared a joke. But soon another woman shared his bed as his wife became pregnant.

They argued about the child. She longed to be a mother, whilst he opposed, making her cry. But then they reconciled and were seen leaving the town by carriage. A short break would do them good.

The next scene was bloody and horrific. The carriage lay on its side and his wife laid face down dead, covered in blood. Bandits circled on horseback and the Mayor stood defenceless. When the leader dismounted, money and laughter were exchanged.

"You disgust me beggar." The visions went, the table became just oak once more and the beggar sat terrified whilst listening. "What sort of man are you? You cannot deny what you have just seen."

By now the sky was virtually black, winds ripped, rain lashed against buildings, whilst others had burst into flames. Bodies scattered the cobbles, broken by the sudden onslaught of elements. Shouts of help became deafened by the wind, which carried them and structures away.

The tavern resembled an overturned anthill. Staff ran here and there, pointing, panicking, not knowing what to do. But the table, chairs, meal and both men, continued undisturbed.

"Why tell you the facts? You know them. Nothing can save your town now beggar, you have failed. It did not take much, a drink of water, a mouthful of food, a kind word. And what came? Nothing." "If you kill them, you must kill me."

Rider laughed. "Kill you. Kill my beggar. I think not. I named you, I created you."

"But…"

"No beggar, you will not die. We had a deal, remember? Your people did not help you. Your people did not speak to you, they were repulsed by you. They did not recognize you. I had to tell them what you were, a beggar." Tutting, Rider waved a hand and the visions returned.

He stood by the overturned carriage and dead wife. A fresh horse had been brought by the murderers. Just as he was about to mount, another man rode into his view. Bright light and a smell of burning engulfed him, swiftly knocking him out.

When the Mayor awoke, the smell had vanished, but the light remained.

"Is this the man?"

"Yes."

"Bring him closer."

Voices could be heard, strange voices, a male and female. Suddenly he moved forward. An unseen force seemed to propel him and two more voices joined the first pair.

"Did we really create it?"

"Of course we did."

"What a mistake."

"They have their good points."

"Name them."

"Silence, silence," a male voice spoke. "Leave your petty squabbling for later. We have a more pressing matter."

"You're right."

"Yes, you're right. Our apologies."

"Time has run its course and still no change." The stronger male voice spoke again.

"And we all agree the action?" A soft female voice asked the question.

"Yes." Many voices, male and female spoke collectively.

"Is he here?"

"Yes."

"He hasn't been used in centuries."

"Centuries or days, he must be used."

"What name does he go by these days?"

"The name he uses is irrelevant. We know his true name."

"Do not speak it." The female spoke.

"No! Do not. *His* name is known to all."

"Ask him to join us."

A silence followed, muffled voices were heard and eventually the new voice came to speak.

"Thank you, thank you friends for inviting me." It was the voice of the man now seated with the beggar.

"I thought you had forgotten me."

"We do not forget *anyone*."

"Especially one such as yourself."

Laughter came and the new voice sounded once more. "So this is him, the Mayor. And of course, the Mayor is in charge of the village."

"We have watched for three generations."

"And no change."

"They have cheated."

"Killed for power."

"Shown no remorse."

"What will the fourth generation be like?"

"They have learnt from the third."

"Then there is no other option."

No one spoke and silence surrounded. "There *could* be a solution to the problem." The voice had suggestion and a hint of menace.

"What do you mean?"

"Be careful."

"Yes be careful."

"Let him speak."

"Thank you. As I said there could be a solution. Give him to me, let me adapt him."

"Adapt him?"

"Yes. If he fails, well, you know what will happen. But should he succeed, the town will be saved."

Many voices spoke, asking questions, debating and finally one voice gave a reply.

"Very well, take him, be gone. We shall wait and hope."

Again the past events vanished, leaving only a flat wooden surface on four legs.

"And here we are beggar, the two of us. After all we have done, the outcome was always inevitable."

"How can you say that?"

"I knew all along beggar. You and your town were doomed from the start."

"No."

"Yes. The long walk across the desert, starving, thirsty, baked in the sun, eventually coming to your town, it was all a game, a game to make things more exciting."

Buildings crumbled against the wind, fire claimed others and the body count mounted. Twisted, broken bodies scattered the ground and blood quickly washed away in the torrential downpour.

White, forked lightning savagely struck the inn, once, twice, three times. Tiles and wood shattered, the roof gave way and flames belched up. The tavern owner rushed out. But a fourth bolt whipped his body, leaving a smouldering charred lump of flesh simmering nicely on the floor.

"Not long now beggar. More lamb?" Rider sat back, looked at his watch and sipped a little wine.

"NO! NO! Stop this madness. I don`t want wine or food…I…I…just want to die."

"Calm yourself beggar. You are not going to die."

"NO!" The beggar swept a forearm across the table, knocking food and wine to the floor.

"Now that was very silly beggar. No need for tantrums and violence."

The beggar fell amongst the scattered meal. Curling up into a ball, he began to cry, pulling at his hair and rags. Breathing became difficult and then he just looked to the sky, lost in a trance, half mad.

Rider stood. Eloquently wiping his mouth, he left money on the table to pay for the meal. Casually walking to the stables, the man returned on horseback. The building collapsed behind him, coughing up dust. Rain ceased and the wind calmed.

Blue sky watched overhead and a warm sun beat down. "Come on beggar, it is time for us to leave." Looking up, tears escaped, but he could not resist. Struggling to his feet, the man clumsily walked forward.

"We have much to do you and I. The next town is not far."

Next town the beggar thought. He wanted to shout out loud, but was unable. He was unable to speak, unable to oppose, unable to resist. He longed for his past life as the Mayor, but deep down knew that now he would always be the beggar. His very soul no longer belonged to him. Casting a quick glance back, he saw the table. It still stood after all that had happened. Birds now feasted on the remaining offerings and a light breeze scattered the money over the corpse of the tavern owner.

"Do you think you might have better luck next time beggar? Mr Sativola thinks so."

Several meows escaped the leather bag. "Yes, I know the lightning frightens you."

Another sound came. "Very well, no lightning next time."

The ruins were left behind, as the small party travelled along the river bank, through woodland and into the mountainous regions. Hours passed, the weather cooled and eventually they became specs on the horizon.

"Look at the stars beggar, what a beautiful sight." Feet just trudged, moving forward, he didn`t bother to look.

"I think we shall make a good trio, I hope so anyway, such adventures ahead of us."

Legs were weary and a mad, glazed expression covered the unwashed man in rags.

"Ah well, it looks like it should be another nice day tomorrow beggar. Do you know any songs? I once knew a man from the south, wonderful singer, shame he..................

The girl with no shoes

The North of England
1983

Summer, July, finally warm weather and blue skies filled the days right through until late evenings. No more school until September and when Dave returned, it would be his `O` level year.

*Ah well, never mind, it was holiday time, exams and worry can wait, I`ve got more important things on my mind.* These thoughts slowly drifted through the fifteen year old`s mind and he smiled.

ΔΔΔ

"What time will you be back?"

"I dunno mum, about half five. I`ll catch the five past bus."

"Well make sure you do. Me and your father are going out tonight and *your* babysitting."

Dave sighed. "Don`t sigh, it`s your turn. And before you ask, your sister isn`t going to stay at grandma`s."

"What about him?"

"Him? You mean Mark, your brother."

"Mmm."

"Mark is going out with his friends for a meal. And don`t pull that face."

"I`m not."

"Stop it."

Dave got that look, that look that said enough or things are going to get a lot worse.

"Sorry."

Dave`s Mum pursed her lips and continued.

"Mark is eighteen now, he`s allowed to go out for a meal or to the pub." There was an uneasy short pause. "He starts University in September and won't be with some of his friends; so they`re all making the most of the holidays together."

Manchester University, that`s right, bye Mark, bedroom to myself. Another thought came as his Mother continued to lecture.

"You could go to University, you're quite capable of getting the results David. Anyway it'll do you good to spend some time with your sister, you've spent the last couple of Saturdays sleeping at Craig's house."

Dave had turned off to the words. He stood, appeared to listen and occasionally nodded his head. He was already somewhere else. The young man, with a rare talent for writing and artwork, had put himself within one of his fictitious worlds. Dave was now standing face to face with a demon; they circled each other, laughed and commenced battle.

ΔΔΔ

The blue Capri 2.8i pulled up outside, Dave's Mum heard the engine and the horn sounded. "Your Dad's here. Take care, see you later."

"Yeah, see you later."

Dave's Dad was dropping him off in town. He'd had to nip into the office to collect some plans he'd left there yesterday. Elizabeth, Dave's sister, had gone with him, then she was going to ballet.

Ballet lessons were always on Saturday mornings at eleven. If their Dad wasn't at work, he would always take Elizabeth to ballet and then they had lunch together as a treat.

Architects, building work, ballet, it all seemed boring to Dave. A little fantasy art or Iron Maiden was his cup of tea. He didn't want to study building design and listen to New Romantic music like his brother and as for ballet, well, it just wasn't him.

Approaching the roundabout, Led Zeppelin's Whole Lotta Love started to play. Dave's Dad turned up the volume. "Now this is proper rock music, a classic."

The middle child said nothing and didn't dispute. Temporary road works had halted the flow of traffic, so he got to listen to the whole track. Iron Maiden's Run to the Hills followed.

This was the "Saturday morning double rock track," played by the local D.J. After that, sounds reverted back to the usual pop tunes and phone in quizzes. By twelve it was news, followed by football chat and commentary on local matches, boring.

The Capri started to move. Dave and his sister both sat in the back, as files and boxes filled the passenger foot well. People looked and admired the gleaming machine, complete with alloys.

The car was only two weeks old. Their Dad`s building company had gone from strength to strength over the last eighteen months and so he had given himself a treat for all the long hours and hard work.

Dave looked out of the window, some people he recognised others were unfamiliar. A mixture of young and old all made their way into town.

"Just pull over outside the cinema Dad, I`ll jump out there."

"Are you sure?"

"Yeah, that`s fine. I`ll walk, it`s not far."

"Alright then."

The volume was turned down and Dave could hear the indicator. His Dad was still speaking, but he`d been distracted. Dave Green was completely lost within himself.

He watched her move, watched her walk along the pavement Who was she? He`d never seen her before, but Dave Green was in love. Tight jeans showed off a nice behind and on top she wore an Ace Frehley T shirt. Dave liked the American rock band and wondered if she was from The Big Apple.

But the strangest thing of all was that she wore no shoes, she was walking bare foot. *Bare foot*, Dave thought, *strange but sexy.*

As the car came to a halt, the young infatuated man almost leapt out.

"Bye, see you later." He quickly spoke and shut the door. She had passed and he hadn`t got a proper look at her face.

Other people looked back, as they passed in the opposite direction, to glance at her bare feet. But Dave just started to follow, taking in the rear view and long dark hair.

Suddenly stopping, she twirled round, glanced at him, smiled, then turned and continued to walk. Dave felt himself blush. He always blushed when girls were around. It wasn`t as if he didn`t like them, or got tongue tied, it just seemed to happen without any warning.

"Hi Dave," the voice spoke getting no reply.

"Ignore me Dave. Bye." Again words came. Dave suddenly snapped out of his trance, spun round and yelled.

"Sorry Claire, miles away. Everything thing ok?"

"Yeah fine, see you Monday."

Claire Haines was just a plain looking girl, who lived with her Grandma. She often came into town, on Saturday mornings, to fetch the shopping. Both were in the same chemistry and physics classes, which Claire thoroughly enjoyed.

Crossing the road, Dave took the back route past the bingo hall, which brought him to the front of the local college.
Passing the main steps, he almost stopped in his tracks and back peddled. With his heart thumping and blushing again, Dave was almost alongside her, alongside the young woman he had been following.

Sitting three steps up with her head tilted back slightly, she smiled and he couldn`t break eye contact.

"Hi," she wasn`t American. "Looks like it should be another nice day."

Time seemed to stop for Dave. "Yeah, should be."

"Off to meet mates?"

"Yeah, we always meet on Saturdays. Have a look round town, records shops and stuff. Sometimes get a video and watch it at Craig`s."

"Have you seen Return of the Jedi yet?"

"Yeah, we`ve seen `em all. Good films."

She nodded, smiling again. What was happening? She must be seventeen, eighteen and Dave was having a conversation with her as if they had known each other for years.

She stretched, moving her head from side to side. As she did so, part of her midriff showed and Dave felt a twinge of excitement.

The young woman, whose name he did not know, ruffled her hair then jumped to her feet. "Well, I`ve got to go."

"Me too, I`ll be late for my mates." Dave replied without blushing.

"Ok. Maybe I`ll see you later."

"Yeah, bye then."

"Bye." Dave started to move, but she hadn`t finished. "What did you say your name was?"

82.

"My name? Er, Dave, Dave Green."

"I'm Louise, Louise Meadows. Most people call me Lou."

"Bye then Lou."

"Bye Dave."

A quick glance and they both went their separate ways. Dave was on a total high. Was he on another planet or in one of his fantasy worlds? He'd just been talking to the "sexiest" woman he'd ever met and she seemed to like him. Wait until Craig Westfield heard about this, Dave thought.

ΔΔΔ

"Coke please, large." He waited until asked what size he wanted before finishing his sentence, "And a cheeseburger."

"Right love, about five minutes. I'll bring it over."

Dave nodded and went to join his mates. They'd been laughing and pulling faces whilst he'd queued and the last mate to arrive had returned the favour.

"Come on Green, where've you been?"

"Greeney, how's it going?"

"Alright lads."

They all greeted each other in the usual manner, laughing, joking, questioning each other's sexuality. The Olympic café was busy, as it always was at Saturday lunch.

All the red leather seats were taken, plates accompanied with cups filled tables and cigarette smoke filled the air. A few old regulars still attended, mostly in their late fifties or early sixties. But the main cliental was no older than twenty.

The shopping centre had recently been revamped and now boasted a new roof, making it all undercover. The café front looked out onto the bus station. People jumped off the single and double deckers, walked past the long glass side, which sat opposite the Gas Showroom, peered in and then cursed at not been able to get a table.

Dave kept joining the conversation as he ate his burger. Craig had finished his meal and now smoked an Embassy No.1, whilst Rick and Pete both tried to read the same Kerrang! Magazine. Martin had taken to rolling his own tobacco and started a second conversation about what everyone's favourite heavy metal track was.

Iron Maiden`s Number of the Beast figured strongly and the band had also charted back in April with Flight of Icarus. Everyone agreed that Joan Jett was a goddess and laughed at the fact that Mike Read has said on air that her song wouldn`t do much.

"He`s a nob."

"Yeah, you`re right Pete. What does he know about music?"

"Not a lot Craig. Tommy Vance should replace him."

"Good idea Martin."

"I agree Rick." Dave took a drink and continued. "I like Creatures of the Night by Kiss."

As Dave spoke, the conversation continued, but he was lost in his own thoughts. He thought about his meeting with Lou and the T shirt she was wearing, which had prompted his last statement.

"They`re not bad for an American band."

"What difference does that make Pete."

Craig questioned him, knowing full well that his friend was very loyal to British bands and always looked for weaknesses in artists from other countries.

"They`re massive in America. Maybe we could start wearing makeup."

"Nice one Rick, just like Twisted Sister." Martin laughed as he spoke.

"Ah Pete! Another band from America. Go on pick fault, pick fault Pete." Craig stood and ruffled his friend's hair.

"Get off lunatic."

"You`re the lunatic Pete."

"Come on, let`s go." Martin stood and the rest followed.

Sharing a joke, all five left. Three or more conversations were going on at the same time, as they passed the Gas Showroom and made their way to the Market.

Dave hadn`t mentioned Lou to anyone yet. The time wasn`t right, so he decided to wait. They were all joking, out to buy records, badges and T shirts. Various girls from school would come into the day and so a little "ribbing" would come about, regarding who "fancied" who.

No, his mind was made up. As the day unfolded, there`d be a

chance to talk to Craig alone. Craig was the oldest of the circle and most "experienced" with girls. Although the two didn`t always see eye to eye, they both had a mutual respect for each other.

"Hi Craig. Ready for the Saturday Night Disco next week?" Craig half smiled and nodded as Alison Blake spoke and the others girls just stood and giggled. But before he could reply with words, she questioned him again.

"What do you think of Mr Spencer the new English teacher?"

"Seems ok. He only started five weeks before the end of term, so it`s hard to tell."

The two were deep in conversation, but Alison was expecting more than Craig. Martin shared a joke with Fiona, their relationship seemed to be on and off frequently, Rick wandered off with Nicola and Pete into Woolworths and Dave just stood, froze and stared.

Oh no! He thought. But then he felt happy, a little giddy and quite excited. Lou walked slowly and effortlessly towards them. She looked fantastic, lithe and seductive, but then again warm and friendly.

Again people stared at the lack of footwear. Dave just became lost within himself. She was gorgeous, forget Joan Jett, forget Sarah Bell from the sixth form and never mind Miss Crossley his Biology teacher, Lou beat them all.

"Hi Dave."

Seconds passed and Dave blushed slightly.

"Hi Lou," he replied nervously.

Nervous, why should he be nervous? And then he blushed again. Dave pushed these thoughts away, took a deep breath and moved closer. Standing as tall as he could, the young man in love spoke again.

"What`s in the bag?" This seemed like a good casual line to start with. Lou smiled, "New knickers and a bra!"

Time seemed to almost standstill, her hand reached inside and his face flushed a lovely red. The black garments came into view, only for a second, then disappeared.

"I`ve got to go Dave, there`s a bus in ten minutes. I`ll see you later." She smiled, "Take care." As these last two words were said, her arm reached up and hands touched. It was only a light touch, hardly anything, lasting a second at the most, but they touched.

"What a freak."

"Yeah, who was that Dave?"

"Can`t she afford any shoes?"

Two of the girls spoke, mocking Lou, then Craig piped up.

"Yeah Greeny, who`s that? Your new girlfriend? People laughed and he continued. "Mind you, she looked alright, might try my luck."

"Hey!" Alison elbowed him.

I don`t think so Craig. She wouldn`t look at you twice, what would she see in you? These words entered Dave`s mind and he became defensive. He suddenly felt strange. For the first time in his life he didn`t want to be with his friends, he wanted to be alone with Lou.

The rest of the afternoon passed quickly and with less conversation about Lou than Dave had expected. The girls spoke amongst themselves, giggling, sometimes casting glances at him. Craig, Martin and the rest did the usual thing. They asked about the lack of shoes, asked about her age and also asked if he`d "done it."

Dave put on a brave face and joked along. Space Invaders soon ate all the ten pence pieces and pockets just housed bus fares. Craig and Dave walked to the bus station together, sharing an Embassy No.1.

"Are your Mum and Dad going out tonight?"

"They went away this morning." Craig replied.

"They`ve gone to York to stay in the caravan. They`ll be back Sunday evening."

"I`ve got to baby sit."

"That`s what big brothers are for." Craig patted him on the back as he spoke.

"Yeah I suppose so."

"Don`t look so sad Greeny. We`re off to Leeds on Monday. Might even see your new mate."

Dave half smiled and thought about how lucky Craig was. No brothers or sisters and parents who left him at home whilst they went away. He always seemed to have money in his pocket, did well at school and had no problem chatting up girls.

I wonder if he could chat up Lou? Probably. As the bus slowly moved through the traffic, Dave asked himself questions about Craig. Then he moved onto Martin and the rest. After two stops, his thoughts moved on to how he would spend the night and then slowly progressed to Monday and Leeds.

ΔΔΔ

Fish fingers, chips and beans went down well. His sister was tired and in bed by half past six, put there by Mrs Green. Dave suffered a half hour lecture on how he mustn't answer the door to strangers, how he had to listen out for his sister, not to spend "hours" on the phone" and if he went to bed before they got back, he must turn off the lights and lock the door.

The white MkII Escort pulled up outside, Mark came down the stairs, shouted bye to everyone and left. Not before his Dad patted him on the back, accompanied with the words "Have a good night son." Their Mother added a kiss and a "take care love, see you in the morning."

Wasn't Mark wonderful? Yes he was in the eyes of Dave's family. Once again Dave discussed life, keeping the questions and answers to himself.

ΔΔΔ

"Another cup of tea would be lovely Lou."
"Coming right up Grandma. And a Kit Kat, I've been shopping."
"Lovely."

Lou smiled as she spoke from the kitchen. The kettle had boiled and the Kit Kats were already out. As the tape recorder clicked off, she quickly pressed eject, reversed the tape and pressed play. Paul Stanley's vocals purred and her latest buy, Kiss Alive II, filled the room.

"Thank you my sweetheart. I do like a nice drink of tea. Madge is coming round on Monday, we're having an afternoon of bridge. Have you…"
"Yes Grandma, there's plenty of gin and the winning bottle of champagne is cooling in the fridge."
"I don't know what I'd do without you," the lady in her eighties

smiled, then continued. "You`re a good girl, just like your mother. She`d be proud of you, very proud of you Lou. And you look *just like her.*"

Tears welled as she took in a deep breath. "I love you grandma." "Ooh! Don`t you get yourself upset. Go on now, leave me alone, I`ll be asleep in an hour."

Lou relaxed, soaking in the bath whilst absorbing Lord of the Rings. AC/DC ruled the air waves, until lukewarm water and wrinkled skin told her it was time to get out.

The Match of the Day theme tune caused her to turn off the telly, football was not top of the list. Tea and toast went down well, along with three more chapters, (Frodo rode on the white elf horse of Glorfindel, escaping the Black Riders). *Wasn`t The Lord of the Rings fantastic,* she thought.

Falling asleep within the comforts of the armchair, she awoke, smiled and found her way to the bedroom. Sleep consumed her again, along with dreams and Lou didn`t awake until sunlight filtered into the room.

ΔΔΔ

Dave got to bed about eleven, his parents weren`t late back. After convincing them that his little sister hadn`t stirred once and telling them he`d taped and watched Knight Rider, he finally escaped.

Sunday morning soon came, bringing more sunshine. Dad made bacon sandwiches, which everyone enjoyed. Dave decided to take a walk, buy a magazine from the newsagents and enjoy a quick cig. Returning about an hour later, the rest of the family had decided to visit Grandma, then return for a "lazy day." The youngest son decided to decline the offer and went upstairs to listen to music.

After two albums, a cheese sandwich and several drinks, the phone rang.
"David…David, phone call for you. It`s Craig."
"Coming Mum."

Thundering down the stairs, he leapt the last three in one. His Dad protested, but words were spoken by their mother. "Calm down love. Sshh quiet now Craig`s on the phone.

"Craig," there was a pause and he continued. "Yeah fine."
Another pause.
"Playing music, haven`t done much today."
Dave nodded several times and smiled. "Course I`m going to Leeds.
About eleven, no problem. See you later. Yeah bye."
"How`s Craig love?" Dave`s mother spoke, enquiring.
"He`s fine."
"Nice boy."
"Mmm." Dave nodded.
"How`s he doing at school David? Do you think he`ll go to
University?"
"Fine, probably." Both questions were answered with a single word.
"We`re going to Leeds tomorrow mum."
"With Craig?"
"And a few others. Martin, Pete, the usual lot."
"What time will you be back?"
"About six. But Craig wants me to stay at his house."
There was a slight pause and Dave took in a deep breath
expecting the worst.
Then his mother spoke. "Well I suppose that`s ok. Ring when you
get to Craig`s though."
"Ok Mum."
"That`s alright isn`t it love?" This was directed at her husband,
who quickly replied.
"Yes, fine. Make sure you phone son."
Sunday afternoon went just like any other. Nothing much
happening, nothing worth watching on television and nobody really
wanting to do much.
Dad messed about with the car for about half an hour, then came
inside to read the newspaper. Mum played with her daughter and
prepared food in the kitchen. Mark returned to a "heroes" welcome
and sat talking with his Dad in the lounge. Dave messed about
drawing and listening to music.

ΔΔΔ

"We seem to have a new postman Lou. I wonder what happened
to the old one?"

"Don`t know gran. The post seems to come earlier though."
"Yes, you`re right love."
The two made polite conversation, whilst eating Sunday lunch. Open dining room windows let in a little air and also gave a splendid view of the rear garden. Both liked the Victorian stone detached house, but little work had been done since they had moved in three months ago.

"I`ll be up early tomorrow gran, I`m going out for the day."
"That`s fine love."
"I`ll bring up your breakfast before I go."
"You don`t have to do that. You get yourself off, don`t worry about me."
"No, it`s no problem. I want to do it. Breakfast will be about eight."
The old lady gave a warm, kind smile and continued with her meal. Lou poured a little more wine for each of them, enjoyed a sip and sliced some more chicken.

ΔΔΔ

Monday brought the warmest day so far. Dave was awake and couldn`t get back to sleep. Six thirty in the morning and he was getting dressed. His Dad stirred, came into the bedroom, looked, then headed for the bathroom.

"Are you going into work today Dad?"
"Course I am Dave. You don`t get long holidays in the "real world."
"The real world? Right Dad."
Mrs Green stirred and soon all three were downstairs and having breakfast. Dave enjoyed his toast, along with a mug of tea.

Smiling, he thought about the day ahead. Leeds with his mates, then back to Craig`s. His parents were going away again, so a small party had been arranged.

Some of the girls were going, they wouldn`t stay the night, but that didn`t matter; girls, music, maybe a few cans of beer and Craig had "acquired" a copy of The Evil Dead on video. All these thoughts flooded Dave`s mind, putting a huge smile upon his face for some time.

"Can you drop me of in town Dad?"
"In town, at this time?"

"It's a bit early David." Mrs Green looked concerned.

"It's not *that* early. I want to get some books from the library before anyone else gets their hands on them."

"Books?" Mr Green looked up.

"Yes books. Books on drawing fantasy art. They told me last week that they'd be on the shelves this Saturday morning. If I leave it 'till later, someone else will pick them up and then I'll have to wait weeks."

His Mum smiled and Dave continued, she knew how much he liked his artwork.

"The library opens at nine, so I want to be the first in."

"What will you do until nine? It'll only be just after eight when I drop you off."

"I'll get a drink at the Olympic Café"

His Dad nodded, whilst his mother just half smiled. Breakfast was soon finished and the two were in the car.

Pulling over just before the traffic lights, Dave jumped out. The journey didn't take long and he was soon seated in his favourite café. Dave quite liked the idea of just sitting and relaxing, whilst drinking a large mug of tea, accompanied by a Kit Kat.

Manual workers were sparse, as most had quickly slurped drinks and left. Rushing to their destinations, they departed with an array of newspapers opened at the racing pages, which were tucked into the backside pockets of their jeans.

A few people in suits remained, they obviously didn't start until nine and squeezed in a second coffee. The remainder was made up of the elderly and unemployed

These two groups always seemed to be present at this time and Dave could never understand why. If he were unemployed or old, he'd stay in bed and relax.

"Hi Dave." As the words flowed, a strange sensation engulfed him. Recognising the voice, he couldn't believe his ears. Turning to look, his eyes did not lie. It was Lou.

"Mind if I join you?"

"No. No not at all."

Dave was slightly embarrassed. There she stood, right as his side.

Smiling, she sat only inches from him. He could nearly feel her body against his.

Looking down, he noticed she wasn`t wearing anything on her feet and her toe nails were painted purple. She wore a matching purple vest, which was covered with a denim jacket.

"Doing anything good today?"

"We`re going to Leeds."

"Leeds," Lou took a long drink of cool fresh milk and continued.

"I like Leeds, lots of good shops."

"You`ve been then."

"Yeah! Loads of times."

"What time are you going?"

"About eleven. A few of us are meeting up."

Lou nodded, whilst drinking, Dave continued.

"I`ve got to call at the library first."

"Can I come?"

"To Leeds?"

"No. To the library. Why would you like me to come to Leeds with you?

"Well… it`s…"

"I`m only joking. I`m sure you don`t want me to tag along when you`re with your mates."

"You can… It`s not a problem."

"No," Lou laughed. "I`ve got things to do. I`ll come to the library though."

Dave was about to speak but got tongue tied. "Calm down. Don`t look so worried, I not laughing at you. You just get all nervous and it makes me laugh."

She gently touched his hand. "Don`t worry, I don`t bite Dave" He didn`t know what to do.

"Come on, let`s go." Lou stood, beckoned with a finger and repeated her words.

"Come on."

As the two walked side by side, others cast glances. Crossing the road, the library came into view and the steps were soon climbed.

"I love libraries." Lou spoke as she soon as she entered and

Dave agreed.

"What are we looking for?"

"Follow me." Dave replied.

He knew the way off by heart and the books was soon found."

"Brilliant." Dave spoke with excitement, "First one to get it."

"Mmm fantasy art."

Dave looked up as Lou spoke and became slightly embarrassed as she had removed her jacket to reveal a curvaceous cleavage and midriff.

He didn`t think she had done it on purpose, she was just the confident, friendly type and he quite liked it.

"Yes, I like to draw. You know, elves, dragons that sort of thing."

"I`m no good at that sort of stuff. I struggle drawing a stick man."

Both shared a laugh and made their way to the desk, to get the book stamped. When they exited and reached the stairs bottom, Lou said a very strange and forward thing.

"Would you like to come home with me Dave?"

He was completely stunned, speechless and unable to think straight. After about six or seven seconds, Dave managed a reply.

"Come home with you. But…"

"Only for half an hour. I`ve got to take some things back for my gran. "

"I`m meeting Craig at eleven."

"The bus only takes ten minutes each way. It`s only twenty past nine now, so we`ll have time to spare."

Smiling, Lou continued. "My gran doesn`t get to meet many people. She`ll be pleased to see you. Then we could play a little music."

"Ok then, fine."

"Good. Come on, the bus leaves in about three minutes."

Running to the stop, they just made it, leapt on and soon sat side by side.

"So where do you live?"

"High Moor Lane."

"High Moor Lane?"

"Mmm," Lou nodded.

"Not in one of those old detached houses."

"Why, what`s wrong with them?"

"Nothing, nothing at all. I`ve always wanted to see inside one of them and hoped you didn`t live in the new houses."

"The new houses. No one seems to like them." Lou laughed.

"No. It was better before they were built, when the old farmhouse still stood."

"And now it`s been knocked down by a developer and lots of money has been made."

"Yeah, something like that." Dave coughed, then continued. "I hope they don`t knock down the detached houses. We`ve been driving past them since I was about five."

"I hope they don`t knock them down either. Not whilst I`m living there." Lou started to laugh and managed another line. " I`d have to come and live with you Dave."

Both laughed together. Lou suddenly jumped up, said it was their stop and the pair jumped off at the middle stop on High Moor Lane.

Dave absorbed the whole scene. After waiting ten years, he was finally going to get inside one of the houses he had endlessly imagined the interior of.

Lou moved two steps ahead, produced a key and open the large door with stained glass. Wasting no time, he stepped inside and the grand staircase, complete with winding banister, welcomed him.

The colour scheme was "just right" and pictures adorned the walls. Looking down he noticed his feet stood on a tiled floor. Various doors were closed to rooms he longed to explore and even the aroma of the dwelling left him with a thirst for more.

"Coke, milk…packet of crisps?"

There was a short pause, then she spoke again.

"Hello! Earth calling Dave."

"Oh! ...Yeah, sorry. Urm, Coke, thanks."

"Well come into the kitchen then."

Dave stood and watched. Lou opened and closed the fridge door, collecting two cans. Opening a cupboard door, a large packet of assorted crisps appeared.

94.

"Help yourself. I`ll have to nip upstairs and see my Gran."

"Okay, fine."

The sound of footsteps ascending filled his ears. Muffled conversation came, followed by footsteps descending. Dave couldn`t really believe what was happening to him and for a moment wished he wasn`t going to Leeds, but could stay here with Lou for the rest of the day.

"She`s fine. Says she`d love to meet you before we go."

"Before we go?"

"Yes, go. Remember, in about half an hour. Why? Would you rather stay here?"

As these words were spoken, she smiled and beckoned him to follow. Was she really asking him to stay? Or was she just fooling around? He didn`t know and followed her into the living room.

"Sit down." Lou spoke, then leapt over the arm of the chair and landed with a thump on her bum. Dave just quietly sat on the sofa.

Lou said nothing, but carefully observed her guest, trying not to smile.

"What?" Dave became embarrassed.

"Nothing, just wondered what you were thinking. What do you want to listen to?"

"Anything, you choose."

"How about a little Kiss?...Creatures of the Night?"

"Fine."

"Oh! It`s upstairs. Come on Dave you can help me get it."

She leapt up and dragged Dave of the sofa. "Come on."

Both went upstairs and soon stood in her bedroom.

It was large with various posters adorning the walls; a dresser, complete with mirror stood by the far wall and a wardrobe adjacent to the door sat with its doors open. The bed was made and purple sheets matched the pillow. On the floor, a uniformed line of vinyl awaited selection to be played on the machine which stood only a foot away.

"Here it is."

Dave just nodded.

"We might as well play it here." Lou spoke, removed it from its sleeve and soon the needle touched.

After a slight crackle, Paul Stanley`s vocals filled the room and Lou sang along with him. Rising to her feet, she drank a little Coke. Spilling down her top, she cursed and moved towards the wardrobe.

Without thinking, Lou removed her vest top. Dave watched and became quite excited. "Oh!" She turned to face him and continued. "Sorry Dave, didn`t mean to embarrass you."

Blushing a bright red, redder than he`d ever gone before, his mouth became very dry and an uneasy sweat covered him.
"Don`t blush Dave, there`s no need to." He couldn`t take his eyes off her, they wandered and she noticed.

Moving slowly towards him, Lou stopped inches away. Her face nearly touched his and soft lips caressed. Dave didn`t respond at first, but Lou continued. Indulging in a sensuous kiss, Dave responded. His hands were guided to her firm supple breasts and Lou enjoyed them being fondled.

Several minutes passed, Dave`s breathing relaxed and he became fully absorbed in the feelings they shared.

Lou let Dave`s hands wander, letting him enjoy her soft, smooth bare flesh. Removing another garment, she now stood naked from the waist up. Again a little guidance was given and Lou licked her own lips in satisfaction as the young man tasted her neck and nipples. Soft words began to flow, along with small groans of pleasure. "I think …you better stay her. Forget Leeds."

She was in control. Pushing him back towards the bed, she, slowly undressed him and he lay on his back. It was as if Lou knew everything, answered questions before he could ask them and knew what he was thinking.

"Relax Dave , she can`t hear us, she struggles on her feet. I have to help her."
Dave swallowed and controlled his breathing.
"I know it`s your first time, I can tell."
He tried to speak, but she just leant over and kissed him. "*Everything* will be fine."

A hand moved to his erection and she smiled whilst whispering in his ear.

96.

"See what I mean, I`ll turn up the music if it makes you feel any better."

Shaking his head, Dave spoke. "No, just leave it."

He couldn`t take his eyes off her and she knew it. They both now lay on the bed, naked except for briefs. Touching, softly speaking, the two became at ease with each other.

Soft gentle hands removed his only item of clothing and removed hers. She smiled, kissed him and comforted with gentle eyes. Excitement, relaxation and happiness engulfed him. Lou gently mounted him and he soon joined the rhythm. Moments later they were laid side by side, listening to music.

When the music finished, silence followed and the two enjoyed a cigarette.

"Shall I put the B side on?"

"Yeah, why not."

Lou slowly moved and made her way to the record player. Dave watched and as the music began, she danced to the rhythm. He beamed, then laughed. Lou just smiled and continued.

"Fancy playing a game?"

"A game?"

"Mmm, a game Dave."

"What sort of game?"

"Trust me, you`ll enjoy it."

"Okay then."

Smiling wickedly, she danced over to the wardrobe. Producing four pieces of rope, Lou glided seductively back and laughed.

"Ready to play?"

Naked, a little nervous and somewhat excited, Dave Green couldn`t really believe what was happening.

"What happens next? I haven`t done anything like this before."

"Wait and see."

Moving to the door, she put on a dressing gown, told him to wait a minute and left the room.

When she returned, he let out a sigh of relief. Again she danced, teasing him.

"What have you got behind your back?"

"Wait and see."

Inching closer, he asked again and she gave the same reply.

"Come on Lou," Dave laughed. "What are you hiding?"

"What am I hiding eh? Do you really want to know?"

"Yes. I really want to know."

"It`s a knife. A knife to cut out your heart."

Fear set in. Dave writhed, eyes widening, he began to scream. Rushing towards him, Lou stuck the blade at his throat.

"Quiet." The word was sharp, menacing and repeated. "Quiet." He wanted to be sick, but then felt like crying. Eyes welled and his nose started to run. Words formed, but wouldn`t escape.

"Pathetic." As she spoke, Lou bent down, picked up a sock and rammed it into Dave`s mouth.

"Stop your whimpering. I can`t bear it."

Looking at his naked form, Lou gently sliced the blade across his midriff; left to right, then right to left, causing a little blood to flow. The taker of his virginity licked the two wounds and seemed to relish the taste.

"I bet your heart tastes delicious. Mmm can`t wait." She let out a deranged laugh, which was cut short when the door flew open.

"Don`t you be having all the fun. What about your gran?"

"Grandma, I was just about to call you."

"So this is the young man is it?"

The grey haired, half blind woman hobbled towards the bed. Smiling, baring the few teeth she possessed, her wrinkled hand brandished a knife. Near milky eyes stared and Dave could almost taste her breath as a hairy chin virtually touched him. Quivering, a cold sweat gleamed on his body and the young man emptied his bladder in fright.

"Let me have a little taste, I`m hungry."

The cold steel sliced across his ribs. Fingers helped themselves, teeth chewed and the rasher of flesh was enjoyed. Dave screamed in agony and ropes cut, drawing blood.

"Mmm, delicious Lou. Here try some." Another slice was taken, Lou refused, so her gran wasted no time.

"So tender, you were right my love, he does taste nice."

"Quiet gran." The old lady looked offended, Lou looked serious. "We`ve waited a long time for this moment. Before he dies, I`m going to tell him."

"Alright dear, you go ahead."

"Dave Green, David Green. You even look a little like him, Charles Blackstock Green. You don`t know who he is do you?" Dave shook his head from side to side, hoping cooperation would bring life.

"You only use the name Green, strange. The Blackstock is no longer used, I wonder why?"

"Strange dear. Mmm, yes." Gran added.

"He was about your age, wealthy, good looking. He desired me, wanted me and had me. He had me against my will. Bastard."

"Yes, bastard." The old lady cut Dave.

"You wanted me Dave and you had me."

"You dirty little bastard." Again the knife cut.

"Gran." Lou shouted.

"Defiling my grandaughter." She sliced the sole of his foot.

"Sorry dear, I just want to eat him. Sorry." She half smiled as Lou glared.

"In fact his father had me too. They all had their *pleasure*. Typical of men. Taking things they want, hurting people. You look confused Dave and you`ve wet yourself."

"Hurrgh! I`ll have to wash those sheets now. You dirty…"
As the knife moved, Lou intervened "Gran."

"You see it all goes back to Henry Blackstock Green. He`s your ancestor, without him you wouldn`t be here."
Lou`s eyes looked full of memories. "He had money, land, power, everything. He married into more money and had a son, Charles. We were about the same age, but lived completely different lives. We lived in the woods, in a small building my father built. They lived in a mansion, with servants."

Dave struggled a little and closed his eyes. Lou looked as though she might cry.

"They hung my father, from a tree. All because he tried to stop them. Such a long time ago now."

"Sixteen forty two, Essex."

"Yes that's right gran. You see Dave we're witches. Me, gran, mother. Father wasn't but he loved us all the same. It's not our fault, we were born this way. We can't help it if we crave for human flesh."

Lou moved nearer, removing the gag and as she did so Dave let out a scream.

"Better? Don't want you dying on us."

"No, don't you die." Gran agreed.

"Please…please don't kill me." Dave finally found words.

"Please, please. Are you pleading for your life?"

"Please Lou…"

"Shut up, you pathetic creature." Lou cut him off mid-sentence.

"My mother pleaded for her life and they mocked her. They mocked her even when she was burning. Gran pleaded when they tortured her. Stand up gran, stand up and show him your legs."

Rising to her feet, the old lady hitched up her skirts to reveal scarred, burnt legs.

"See, look at them. Henry did that. After he'd hung my father, he tortured gran, tried to make her confess. Then he turned on my mother. I loved my mother. His wife was a sour faced bitch who gave him nothing in the bedroom, so he thought he could have my Mother. But it all started with me and Charles. That spoilt brat always had his eye on me. His friends held me down and he had me, but I scratched his pretty face. Not long after they arrived, Charles, Henry and the rest. What chance did my father have?"

"Oh God, please God no." Dave cried as he spoke.

"Shut up and listen to my grandaughter. You dirty little bastard."

"We had to watch as they took it in turns with my mother. Then they hurt gran. Charles laughed, encouraged by his father, as he had his pleasure with me again. Only this time mother had to watch."

"But I knew a spell, didn't I gran?"

"You did my dear, you did." The old lady beamed with pride as she spoke.

"NO! NO! Lou, let me go, you need help."

"Help, help?" Lou's mood changed.

100.

"We needed help." As each word was spoken, she sliced his body. "And none came."

Dave screamed. Quivering on the sheets, blood ran over his bare torso, staining the bed.

"You`re all the same, not satisfied with what you have, you think you can take something that doesn`t belong to you. I had to watch my mother burn, found guilty of been a witch. But that didn`t stop them having her did it? "

"Lou…please…ple…"

"You destroy what you don`t understand. Can we help the way we are born. We only killed thieves and murderers who hid in the forest. Father helped us. We kept ourselves to ourselves. But in the end it all comes down to lust, desire, flesh. Henry had wanted my mother for a long time and his son felt the same about me."

"That family has always been the same, ever since they came to Essex."

The old lady twirled the blade in her hands, looking distant. Taking a deep breath she continued.

"Evil, corrupt people, whole lot of them."

"Don`t upset yourself gran. Everything going as I said it would."

"Yes your right dear."

"You see Dave," Lou sat on the bed, running a finger up and down his body.

"They decided to hurt me, punish me. They hung me from one of the beams in the barn and whipped me, whipped me hard until I fell unconscious. I can still *hear* and feel the whip now".

Turning, Lou showed Dave her pale, slender back for the first time which bore the lash marks of her whipping.

"The freezing water awoke me and they laughed before whipping me more. But I beat *them*, escaped them "

Dave watched, wide eyed and petrified. Smiling, she kissed him and ran a finger up his naked torso.

"I couldn`t save mother, she was already dead. But I had become powerful, the strongest in our bloodline for centuries. I tried the spell and it worked. Me and gran escaped, vanished before their very eyes."

Lou slowly cut his arm. Driving the blade deep, she whispered. "And now we`ve found you." Again she drove the blade inwards. Dave let out a cry of pure suffering and eyes bulged due to the torture.

"Ten years it`s taken. Ten years to find you. But we`ve learnt, educated ourselves in this strange time. When we first appeared, we barely recognised our surroundings. But a nice elderly couple took us in, took pity on us. They thought we were simple, gypsies folk and didn`t ask questions."

Dave`s eyes flickered, he drifted in and out of consciousness and Lou grabbed his hair tightly.

"Stay awake, Mr David Green. Your heart will soon be mine."

"That nice elderly couple had never met us before, but they accepted us. They gave us clothes, food and shelter. I was educated through books and gran was able to rest and enjoy the nice summer days."

Dave coughed weakly, he just lay on the bed staring.

"When they died we inherited the house. We had wealth and a home. But we always had one thing on our minds and we eventually found you, here in Yorkshire."

Lou stood before him. Smiling, she wielded the knife. The cold steel ran up and down his body.

"I can hear your heart beating." She laughed "Your bloodline will be wiped out, all of you."

"My sister…no...not her."

"Ah, your sister. I`m glad you`ve mentioned her. We`re not really interested in your mother, she`ll probably commit suicide or end up in a mental hospital. Mark and your father will suffer the same fate as you. Lou massaged her breasts. "I`m sure they won`t be able to resist. It runs in the family."

"Please Lou not…not my sister."

"Your sister is very special. You see Dave, Henry Blackstock Green had a secret and this secret has come to our attention. His great grandfather married a witch. Witch blood is in your family. Unfortunately all of the girls born didn`t live beyond the age of three. But your sister is the first in centuries to reach nine and she will become very powerful. "

"NO! NO!...NO!" Dave let out screams of disbelief.
Both woman laughed mockingly. "When she joins us, the coven will
be complete again."

"Fucking bitches. You fucking BITCHES."
"It`s witches you dirty little boy, witches." The old lady cut his
cheek and Dave screamed.

"See how you react, violently, like all men when you don`t
understand. In fact it was your sister who led me to you."
"No, no way."
"Yes. We searched and came across her quite by accident. But when
tested she passed and it just confirmed what we already knew."

"A very nice little girl. I like her."
"You`ve met her? Dave looked at the old lady.
"*Oh yes*, no one can resist an old grannie at ballet. They all love me
to bits."

Dave began to cry. Writhing and pulling as hard as he could, he
tried to break the ropes. But a soft hand touched his chest and pushed
him down. Climbing onto the bed, Lou sat across him. Her soft lips
kissed him passionately and she relished the feeling. Suddenly she
stopped, tossed her head back and spoke in a calm seductive voice.

"I quite like you Dave, but you have to die. You see it was your
sister who told me what you do on Saturdays, which café you like
and so on. When she told me about your taste in music, I knew you
wouldn`t be able to resist. She even spoke to me on that first
Saturday morning, when you were in the car listening to the radio."
"Spoke to you? I don`t understand."
"No, you`ll never understand. She spoke in my head, a witch has
many talents."

Eyes met, smiling, she proceeded to lick his naked torso.
Reaching his mouth, Lou kissed him. For a moment he was lost,
relaxed, engulfed in the seductive moment.

"Goodbye Dave." The words were warm and caring. Pain
stabbed, slicing, cutting. Warm blood ran and his life ebbed away.
The witches laughed, then relished in the tender organ.

ΔΔΔ

All eyes looked at Dave. Everyone looked at his face. Mrs Green was comforted by her husband, tears flowed and he embraced her.

"Where`s Mark?" Words came in between tears.

"Making us all a nice drink of tea."

Mrs Green looked at her son`s face again, he stared back and Sue Lawley continued with the broadcast about the schoolboy who hadn`t been seen in six days.

"Where`s my baby? Lizzie, Elizabeth."

The little innocent girl came running in and cuddled into her mother`s arms.

"Don`t worry mummy, I`m here now."

Mrs Green broke down and couldn`t reply. All three shared a moment on the sofa and Mr Green turned off the T.V. Mark entered and joined them, along with a tray of drinks.

"The University called." Mark spoke. "I don`t have to start on the eighteenth. They`re ringing back tomorrow."

His Dad nodded, "Okay son, thanks."

"I`ll speak to you later Dad, when Mum`s asleep."

Again his Dad nodded and half smiled.

ΔΔΔ

"How far is Manchester?"

"It`s only about forty odd miles gran. I`ll come back most weekends."

"What are you doing at University again?"

"I`m studying History and English."

"Well you take care."

Lou turned to face her only living relative and laughed. "I`m quite capable of looking after myself."

"I know you are dear. Come here and give me cuddle"

The two embraced and Lou spoke softly. "There`s one thing I miss though."

"What`s that dear?"

"Wearing shoes."

Her gran pulled her in tight. "I`m sorry dear, we can`t help that, it`s part of the spell. If you wear any type of footwear, you know you'll be taken back. Back to the very torture you escaped. Only this time you won't be able to escape and you'll take me back with you."

"I know gran, I'm sorry."

Lou continued to pack and the old lady sat and watched, smiling.

"I'm going downstairs Lou. I've got guests, were having an afternoon of bridge."

"Alright gran, I'll pop down later and speak to them."

The suitcase was finally packed and Lou lay on her bed, smoking a cigarette. I Stole Your Love, by Kiss played and she admired the photo of Dave Green in her hand. As the track came to an end, she put a flame to the picture and tossed it into the ashtray.

The seductive young woman smiled, almost letting out a laugh. She opened a drawer and produced another photograph. Caressing it slowly, lips kissed the two men, but they did not respond. She kissed them again, but Mr Green and son Mark kept the same pose. Lou closed her eyes. Holding the picture close to her chest, Joan Jett and the Blackhearts belted out I Love Rock and Roll.

Ribskillian

Written

by

David

Driver

Picture Glossary

Front cover *Tales for the Traveller* by Akiko Kobayashi

Back cover *Story Time Gathering* by Akiko Kobayashi

Page 3 *Jadwiga* by Red Lens

Page 54 *Kalakorn Prison* by Akiko Kobayashi

Page 55 *Laura* by Akiko Kobayashi

Page 56 *Shesha* by Akiko Kobayashi

Page 57 *Louise Meadows* by Akiko Kobayashi

Page 58 *Rider and Mr Sativola* by Akiko Kobayashi

Page 59 *Eveline Mangle* by Akiko Kobayashi

Page 60 *For Sale* by Akiko Kobayashi

Page 104 *Quill and Ink* by Red Lens

The End

Made in the USA
Charleston, SC
26 August 2016